Tales of El Huitlacoche

MAIZE Press

The Colorado College
Colorado Springs, CO 80903

Tales of El Huitlacoche

Gary D. Keller

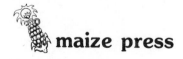 maize press

ISBN: 0-939558-05-X

Library of Congress Catalog Card Number: 83-062552

PRINTED IN THE UNITED STATES OF AMERICA

Cover design by Christopher J. Bidlack

Acknowledgments

Three of the stories in this collection originally appeared in the following publications:

"Papi Invented the Automatic Jumping Bean" (original title, "The Man Who Invented the Automatic Jumping Bean") in *Bilingual Review*, I, 2 (1974). Reprinted in *The Pushcart Prize, II: Best of the Small Presses*, ed. Bill Henderson (New York: Pushcart Press, 1977).
"The Mojado Who Offered Up His Tapeworms to the Public Weal" in *Hispanics in the United States: An Anthology of Creative Literature, Vol. II*, ed. F. Jiménez and G. Keller (Ypsilanti, MI: Bilingual Press, 1981), 13-27.
"Mocha in Disneyland" in *Hispanics in the United States: An Anthology of Creative Literature, Vol. I*, ed. G. Keller and F. Jiménez (Ypsilanti, MI: Bilingual Press, 1980), 57-74.

MAIZE Press
The Colorado College
Colorado Springs, CO 80903

Table of Contents

In memory of
Gilbert Weatherbee
Magister Dixit

The Comic Vision in
Tales of El Huitlacoche

Rosaura Sánchez

The four tales of El Huitlacoche (Gary Keller) included in this volume could be said to constitute a macrotext in that there is a common thematic and formal element running through all the texts that provides unity to the collection. All of the stories deal with a United States-Mexico border situation (even when the border extends to Mexico City itself) and depict the socio-historical and linguistic heterogeneity of the Chicano/Mexicano population. Three of the stories constitute a second unitary text, or macrotext, in that there is a progression in the discourse of one Huitla, the protagonist and implicit author, whose life is traced from early childhood in Juárez, Mexico, in the "Automatic Jumping Bean" story, to a bus ride through the Southwest during his college years in the "Mojado" story, and on to adulthood, parenthood, divorce, and a professional career in the "Mocha" text. The fourth story, although dealing with a Chicano college student, offers a different narrative discourse, as we shall see, and no longer retains the irony and laughter that characterize the Huitla of the other three stories.

The outstanding feature of El Huitlacoche's stories is a burlesque style and a comic vision that serve to reveal the absurdity of human existence and the contradictions of society. Here we find anti-heroic characters, sometimes pícaros or schlemiels, in the midst of a racist, classist, capitalist society. The ironic and humorous treatment of characters and situations allows the author to avoid a passive, "readerly" presentation of Chicano life in the Southwest while at the same time leading the reader to make critical observations of the narrated historical situation. Throughout the stories, El Huitlacoche has chosen to focus on the impact of various social and economic contradictions on the individual through the use of exaggeration, grotesque descriptions, and humorous discourse. Thus, while externalizing fears, repressions, and human bodily acts, the author exposes social conventions, racist/class relations, capitalist labor practices, and the exploitation of undocumented workers in every sphere of American society. The border thus becomes El Huitlacoche's Macondo, an area of bilingual endeavors where the "rogue" can survive by playing both within and outside of the legal system, while the naive dreamer is easily crushed.

In the narrative world of *Tales of El Huitlacoche* there is a steady stream of the comic element, parody, and irony to provoke laughter at the social and economic systems' contradictions. Often the laughter is close to pain as a time-space of pathos crowds the fringes of the comic. The burlesque narrative tone is achieved through the use of a combination of linguistic varieties and styles. This linguistic diversity is especially evident in the dialogues involving the first-person narrator—Huitla—and other characters. The autobiographical discourse assumed in the narration makes for a more intimate and familiar narrative style as if to allow the reader an insider's view of the community. The intercalation of a Spanish popular variety laced with caló within a standard English rendition of the tales makes for a richer literary code and allows for a multiplicity of reading levels: the serious, the indecent, the obscene, the grotesque, and the ridiculous. Each speech variety contains as well a particular point of view identified with the addresser and a particular semantic and social space.

The varied codes evident in the dialogues are an important element in the portrayal of the various characters as well as in the staging of scenes and settings. The secret of the comic vision in *Tales of El Huitlacoche* is, of course, in the textual discourse. Thus in each verbal interaction between father and child or between young males, the tone, phraseology, and use of slang and code-switching are appropriate for the portrayed roles, domains, and topics of conversation. The camaraderie and affection between father and son, for example, as they stop to wrestle at the beach is well captured in their bantering teasing. The code-switching adds a distinctly Spanish flavor to the text and has enabled the author to succeed in reproducing a male Chicano speech style while writing almost entirely in English. The narrative world is, in fact, almost exclusively male; there are few female voices to be heard here.

Like other literary texts, El Huitlacoche's tales establish links with literary codes and conventions and refer to other semiotic systems, thereby enriching the stories' intertextuality. References are thus made to a number of cultural, literary, and historical codes, as is evident in the incorporation of the humorous style of the tall tale, the images of picaresque episodes, and the burlesque realism that recalls the work of García Márquez. In revealing racy details of rural sexual play, suggesting latent incestuous drives, providing ironic portrayals of the border economy where survival often requires the production of nonsense items to sell to gullible American tourists, describing the training of geese as junkyard watchdogs, and detailing the continuous entry/re-entry south, north, and south again of contraband parrots, marihuana, or batteries, the author counterposes the ridiculous and the petty to the disproportionality inherent in a stratified society. The presence of the undocumented worker in the United States, for example, although humorously revealed, is directly contrasted with a capitalist reality where the indocumentado creates a whole network of border jobs, from the numerous Border Patrol officers, the construction crews hired to set up the Tortilla Curtain, the judges before whom the mojados appear, and the centers where they are detained, to the industries where they are hired. Their presence reaches offices and homes throughout the country in the form of a contraband parrot, commodities produced by undocumented labor, or agricultural products picked and packed by wetback hands. The mojado's participation in the economy thus produces profit for American industry and employment for a number of American citizens, as the text humorously asserts.

Texts, then, refer to other texts, whether these be cultural, social, or literary. While these references may vary from story to story, there is one constant intertextual referent: History. El Huitlacoche's tales refer not only to contemporaneous history but to previous history, particularly Mexican history. There are also references to characters in literature (such as Demetrio Macías), to other works and authors (especially from Spanish and Mexican literature), and to popular culture (TV programs and popular music). A good example of a cultural and social referent is the sketch of the border practice of commercial schemes, à la big business, in the episode narrating the application to contraband of the "wet warranty," guaranteeing delivery of contrabanded material to the clients. Caló itself becomes part of the intertextual process, for it is a code representing a particular masculine/youthful/jive-oriented/sexually-connotated humor and perspective that characterize the pícaro who is able to survive as much by scoring and selling Arizona saguaros to business and bank offices as by obtaining a CETA grant to work with ex-junkies training geese as junkyard watchdogs. The sprinkling of loan words, as in the case of the deadly "huevos whateveros," the concoction of egg-scrambled leftovers responsible for the tapeworms in the "Mojado" story, further situates the bilingual/bicultural border context. References to particular commodities also lead to incongrous and humorous situations as in the case of the naive fieldworker who attempts to cross the Rio Grande with snorkel, flippers, diving mask, and plastic trident while the waiting border patrol officers on the other side collapse from laughter.

Laughter and comic exaggeration, although distorting on one level, also create a distance from the border situation that allows for criticism of practices taken for granted in a modern capitalist society. What could speak more strongly about workers' alienation and exploitation than the image of a defecating human machine at the service of science and technology? Thus the grotesque and humorous level is cleverly intertwined with the historical level, producing thereby a dominant ironic tone that permits a manifestation of existing contradictions between the objective and the subjective, the internal and the external, the historical and the burlesque.

"Papi Invented the Automatic Jumping Bean" is the humorous sketch of a Chicano schlemiel, an urban tinkerer-technician, alchemist of sorts like Colonel Buendía, a "clap-trap genius" who invents the automatic jumping bean from a Contac capsule and a ball of mercury "siphoned off a store-bought thermometer" without receiving any recognition or profit from the American company which immediately mass-produces and markets the toy throughout the Americas.

The story begins by recounting the creation of the ridiculous invention and stresses the commercial success of the item in an exaggerated style that recalls Mark Twain's numerous tall tales, particularly the story of the notorious jumping frog of Calaveras County. But the story shifts all too soon from parody to pathos as we face the narrator-son's assessment of a series of his father's "failures" and his passive resignation in the face of a "succession of unprincipled ruses that were played upon my father's person to the discredit of the family honor." This jack-of-all-trades but expert-at-none is an urban character residing in Ciudad Juárez, Mexico, a constant commuter across the U.S.-Mexico border who served in the U.S. Army during World War II and whose children will end up with university degrees—passports, as he calls them—and professional jobs in the United States. But the father is an outsider, an inventive genius outside the mainstream of capitalist production, a creative man alienated from his product and unable to battle the mammoth goliath of big business. Far from being the hero of an idyllic world, our inventor is ridiculous, pitiful, and unnecessary. Before modern technology he stands not as an acerbic Pito Pérez nor as a good-natured and naive Cantinflas going against middle-class conventions but as a frustrated and fatalistic inventor making not marvelous cages but useless gimmicks and novelties.

The time-space of the tall tale with its hyperbolic tribute to the inventor is sharply intersected by historical time. Thus alongside the tinkerer-technician are other workers within an international secondary labor market, toiling in small shops and plants, extracting lead from old Delco batteries, molding it into ingots to be resold across the American border and detinning cans for local industries. Our inventor is a low-income tenement resident in Juárez in 1953, the decade of "Operation Wetback" when thousands of Mexicans were deported and American conservatism and McCarthyism ran rampant; this historical context will later intersect the "Mojado" story as well.

In the midst of this economic situation the father seeks to establish a family enterprise to bequeath to his sons, although he constantly has to face fierce competition from major companies and economic and technological changes that make the processes he has developed obsolete. Yet despite the odds and despite his lack of credentials, he initiates a number of enterprises, each a harebrained scheme worthy of a dreamer-technician:

> How my old man had faith! And he'd been in and out of so many operations. He had scoured the Southwest for old batteries to haul across the border to transform into lead ingots and sell back to the Americans; he had stamped out Jesus Christs on metal

plate, struck Virgin Marys from rubber molds, learned the ins and outs of libraries in order to invent a process to detin cans; he had set diamonds, manufactured brass buttons for the armed forces, designed costume jewelry, set up a nickel-plating bath, run a route of gumball machines, managed a molino de nixtamal for tortillas, bought a chicken farm (without having read Sherwood Anderson), gone to school at the Polytechnic, bred rabbits, trained geese to be industrial watchdogs, raised a family and invented the automatic jumping bean.

He faced the failure of each of these enterprises with passive resignation and fatalism. His son decried his "boundless and totally unfounded faith in people" although he also found his father's response to be "the norm, therefore tolerable" and characteristic of his generation. The son's resentment is as exaggerated as his father's "failure."

In the end the tall tale space is not sustained and the historical level takes over after a brief sketch of barrio life and a description of the father's subjectivity. While presenting the sketch about the pork rind hanging at the chicharronería, the people queueing up for masa at the molino de nixtamal, and Mexican golden-age movies featuring Pedro Infante and Jorge Negrete, the narrator-son recalls his father's fears. The camaraderie between the two after beer and ice cream turns to anguish as the son senses his father's inner turmoil and his lack of a realistic assessment of his true situation. Only in his father's moody periods does the son sense the former's victimization. But even here the existentialist melodrama is offset by the provocative symbol: the image of a "crucified frog" pinned out for analysis on a biology lab table, a perturbing symbol, it seems, for the idealistic father.

After projecting the image of the dismembered frog, the narrator enters the time-space of objective reality wherein industrial accidents at the detinning plant lead to the loss of a worker's leg and to his father's disfigurement by a geyser of caustic soda. The father's idealistic projects to transform dross into gold and his life into something meaningful are thus squelched by objective reality. His sons, however, will go on to college and one will eventually make it as an engineer and work for General Dynamics, where he will help design real submarines, not the toy ones that his father never successfully launched.

In the end, laughter turns to pain for the father. And even while the narrator recognizes that had his father been white, he might have achieved some measure of success or recognition, he looks back not so much with bitterness or resentment as with nostalgia to a period of crazy but creative inventiveness, a period before their credentials brought he and his brother "success" and membership in the professional and consumer society of the United States.

"The Mojado Who Offered Up His Tapeworms to the Public Weal" is a modern picaresque tale wherein the exploitative economic and political structure of the Mexican-U.S. border is sharply exposed through the story of an undocumented worker who migrates back and forth between the two countries. The wetback's life, told in all its Rabelaisian details, is a comic and ironic portrayal of his struggle for survival in the land of plenty. The story offers a parodied hybridization of two time-spaces and perspectives—the documentary accounts of newspapers, films, and novels (such as Spota's) that trace the plight of the undocumented worker, and the picaresque "rogue on the road" time-space—to produce a parody of the "rites of passage" of a mojado who manages to survive on the border despite the assiduity of the Border Patrol, the economic policies of the multinationals and banks, and the game-like river contraband process itself to become a unique public servant: "a worm factory or some kind of one-man maquiladora."

The story in effect begins by positing two dimensions: that of the narrator and implicit author, El Huitlacoche, "on the road" from Texas to California by bus where he meets Rompeculos, and that of the Mojado "on the road" from the fields of Sinaloa to the Juárez border, where he becomes a successful border bandit, and thence to his life as an undocumented worker in the Southwest. The Mojado's story is told in all its grotesque details by Rompe, who assumes a schizoid persona to tell what is in fact his own story, although it is not until the end of the tale that we learn that Rompeculos and the wetback are the same person. The naiveté of the mojado is constantly counterposed to Rompe's shrewd eye and filtered through Huitla's skepticism and delight in Rompe's racy account, which at times is uncharacteristically literary and otherwise sophisticated, calling forth both Huitla's and the reader's suspicions:

> "Did you go to college?"
> "Hell no! ¿Y por qué lo preguntas?"
> "I don't know. You seem so awfully knowledgeable. . . ."

In the initial bus encounter, Huitla, a college student who has just failed to score some mota in Mexico to bring across the border in order to pay his junior year in college, meets a fellow passenger, Rompeculos, who advises him to get into the parrot contraband business instead. As the bus travels through familiar Southwest territory from Texas to Arizona and on to San Diego, the narrator and passenger move from one theme (contraband) to another (Rompe's labor history) while they drink sangrita and tequila and look out the window until Rompe initiates the wetback story.

The story weaves historical and socio-political events together with the personal and grotesque so that in each case we come to see the comical and ridiculous as determined by historical reality. The humorous treatment of the mojado's plight, which follows him from the fields of Sinaloa to a border life of contraband, to the production of tourist novelties and guided tours to local brothels, to the anonimato of an undocumented worker in the garment industry, and finally to tapeworm entrepreneur, allows for a distortion of the subjective and an externalization of the character. In externalizing his virtues and shortcomings the author also exposes the exploitation of undocumented workers throughout the Southwest and the gringo control of the border economy. In presenting the meanderings of the wetback (or, as he is variously called, wettie, mojao, mojado, etc.) with relation to the Border Patrol, state institutions, industry, other border bandits, American tourists, and so on, the text articulates a clearly critical position with respect to discriminatory, exploitative, and contradictory policies affecting the undocumented labor force.

"Mocha in Disneyland" is a continuation of the Huitla macrotext. Unlike the first two stories, where an ironic tone dominates the text, this story is schmaltzy, for here pathos overrides the burlesque. The narrator and his young son, members of the Chicano order of the golden carp (ref. Rudolfo Anaya), seek refuge and testworthiness in a treehouse one night at the world's great capitalist fantasyland. Naked and wet after having swum the channel between Tom Sawyer Island and Fantasyland while fleeing from Disneyland patrol hounds, Pancholín, alias "Mocha"—"the fruit of coffee with milk"—and his university professor father take refuge in the treehouse. The story begins with this night in the Swiss Family Treehouse and ends with their being discovered the next morning by the guards. The final dialogue has Huitla trying to explain the foolish escapade to his ex-wife Linda as he asks her not to go to the judge with the story of his getting booked for trespassing and indecent exposure.

The core of the story is Huitla's recalling the events which led to the night of adventure with his son. Through this subjective discourse we come to sense the malaise of the middle-class Chicano professional who is suffering a mid-life crisis, divorced and separated from his son, and living in a gabacho university world full of proposals for federal grants, audits, and reports. Huitla is by now the "senior Chicano in the State [university] system," with dreams of a possible deanship, but unable to see his son as often as he would like and unable as well to face his Anglo ex-wife's affair with an Anglo "beach bum." Both problems lead to his retreat into a world of fantasy, myth, and continual teasing as he tries to express his love for his son and to instill in the child a sense of security and a notion of Chicano roots and ties. As in the previous stories, the alienation and racism of modern society are dealt with at a subjective level so that again it is the effect and impact on the individual on which the text will focus. The socio-political context is clear but the individual's inadequacies and his lack of objective analysis become the central theme. In the end the professor's laughter is more painful than funny.

"The Raza Who Scored Big in Anáhuac" is part of the macro-text only in that it too deals with the problems affecting Chicanos. Here the life sequence of Huitla is broken, at least in terms of the narration. The main character in this story is not the assertive Huitla trying to score Irapuato green and able to jive with the best of them as in the wetback story; here we find a naive but non-humorous character trying to explain his disillusionment with his search for "roots" but unable to go beyond a feeling of mortification at his own ingenuousness, yet struck with a case of nostalgia for the past.

Throughout the story the student's solipsistic self-pity contrasts sharply with the objective historical reality that continually intersects the text. The two opposing time-spaces—the subjective and the objective—create a contradictory discourse that allows the author the opportunity to play with a number of culturalistic notions that have plagued the Chicano student movement and also to poke fun at them.

"The Raza Who Scored Big" is the melodramatic memoire of a Chicano student in Mexico City who gambled at the Jai Alai with luck, scored gonorrhea after his good fortune gambling, and became disillusioned about the possibility of Mexicano-Chicano compañerismo after his experience with a Mexican hustler-type at the UNAM. The Chicano student's naive expectations and self-pity are contrasted throughout the story with the bleak reality of penniless Mexican Indian students who walk to the capital from as far away as Yucatán to initiate their university careers in a city of 17 million where unemployment is as high as 50% and scholarships for room and board are unavailable.

Like other Chicano university students affected by the culturalist movement, "el güero Valín" takes a trip back across the Río Bravo to seek his roots in Mexico. His vision of Anáhuac, however, although not that of an amazed Spanish conqueror, is definitely that of an outsider reveling in the sights, flattered by his contacts, and impressed by student political rhetoric. Throughout the story the Chicano student is unable to examine his own situation objectively in terms of his economic and political status. Whatever his illusions about his roots and despite his lower-income status in the States, he is a "gringo" in Mexico, with the means to feed his friends, wear "preppie polo shirts," and pay his room and board while at the university. He is thus a prime candidate for a bit of deception and hustling, like any other tourist in Mexico from the imperialist metropolis.

The Chicano student's loss of faith in a "binational carnalismo" is of subjective origin and stems from his being tricked by his friend Felipe Espinoso into betting all his room and board money on a Jai Alai contest. Although they are fortunate enough to win, the "güero Valín" later discovers that all the money bet was his own, that Felipe had nothing to risk and everything to gain from such a venture, and that Felipe, who had been highly critical of the petty bourgeois professor who lectured on the need for social change, saw him not as a carnal but as a potential sucker. In the end the Chicano student is reduced to the subjective, existentialist affirmation of his identity; his consolation is to think himself peerless—no image can reflect his own—and strong in his isolation and estrangement, à la Hemingway: "I am strong where I've been broken and I'm not prepared to cave in."

In the end, while reminiscing at a Cal State library, the student finds comfort in the thought of a transitory communion between "two oprimidos of such divergent estirpe, of such varied formation," as if the two students had been similarly oppressed, as if the poverty-stricken Indian campesinos who came to study, slept under the stairs or in the swimming pool, wore the same guayabera every day of the week, attended classes at the UNAM where there were 260,000 in attendance at a university built for 120,000, "begging and hustling and working" to survive, were at the same level of oppression as a Chicano student with money to travel to Mexico City to relearn the language and gain a mythic "culture." The Chicano is a foreigner there, looking for Vasconcelos' "raza cósmica," a tourist euphoric at a Jai Alai spectacle and at the thought of being one with the countryfolk filling the city for the Virgin of Guadalupe pilgrimage and the stadium for some heavy betting. When the Chicano wavers about betting all his money, Felipe assures him: "Come now, compis. It's not every day that a vato loco can wager with the people with a firm hand." The Chicano student confuses gambling with a revolutionary spirit, attention with friendship, and national origin with class. As Felipe says: "You're poor like Cheech and Chong. We use the same word, poor, but we don't mean the same referent. I mean devastated, a nullity without the remotest identity."

As he reviews his "learning experience" in Mexico City, the Chicano student recalls the many ways in which he was used by Felipe; in the end he mocks his hope for a binational compañerismo and for the possibility of collective action, convinced by his personal experience that all relationships eventually deteriorate into oppressor-oppressed dyads. His need to continue conversing with the Mayan head in the university library art book is the only hint that the student will continue dialoguing with himself in order perhaps to eventually analyze his own contradictions.

All four stories thus offer a combination of the grotesque,

the ridiculous, the melodramatic, and the pathetic to reflect the major contradictions of Chicano society at both the objective and subjective levels. The author's literary discourse is uniquely humorous and offers an internal endo-group perspective, linguistically and culturally, of life in the Southwest. It is his comic vision that makes the absurd and the melodramatic tolerable while at the same time revealing critically an intolerable reality that feeds on human sweat and labor, thereby exposing the social and psychological ills of our time.

UNIVERSITY OF CALIFORNIA,
SAN DIEGO

Papi Invented the Automatic Jumping Bean

My dad invented the first authentic wormless Mexican jumping bean with an empty Contac capsule and a ball of mercury he siphoned off a store-bought thermometer. He did it for potential profit in Ciudad Juárez in 1953 in a high-rise complex that the government built for el pueblo out of prefab concrete and reinforced plastic girders. They named it Huertas de Nezahualcóyotl after the Aztec poet-king.

It was a big seller all over Mesoamérica. I saw it in the heart of Aztlán, through the frosted glass of a candy store window in Alamogordo on Christmas Eve. Big novelty! All-purpose wormless jumping bean! Never dies or runs out on you! Works on body heat! It was in one of those candy stores that the Coca Cola company moves into in a heavy way. They put up all your signs for you. They tack up tantalizing murals of cheeseburgers and coke. Above the counter the name of the store and the proprietor is in lights with two psychedelic Coca Cola imprints on either side, like Christ between his thieves. They only let you sell Coke.

I saw them in the hands of esquintles on the Mexican altiplano and even in the capital. The jobbers on Correo Mayor sold them by the gross to the peddlers, hustlers and other street people. Years later on one of my wanderings I spotted them in the renowned Quetzaltenango market in Guatemala. An old Indian woman in her shawl had them stacked up in symmetrical mounds like frijoles pintos. She looked like one of those sibylline old indígenas from whom one might expect sage or psychedelic advice. I questioned her. "Mother! What do you sell here? Mexican jumping beans?" But she paid me no heed. She sat there, mute and sassy, receiving the indrawn vision.

Not that my old man made a centavo from his invention. That

day in '53 he came home from across the border with only about fifteen Delco batteries in his pickup. Competition was getting brutal. And what with the invention of aluminum cans . . . He had himself two Carta Blancas, scratched himself here and there; then came an inspiration. From the souvenir shelf he took the miniature Empire State building that he had bought on Times Square after the War (fighting for Tío Sam was the thing to do in those days) and carefully removed the thermometer from the tower. Then he came out of the john with a Contac capsule that he had emptied. He split the thermometer and tapped the jelly-like mercury. He made a ball from the mercury and slid it into the capsule. He held the capsule tight between his palms. He looked like he was hiding a cigarette butt from the vicissitudes of the wind. Then he let it go on the table. Mother of God! Did it jump! My father, who was fond of scientific discourse (he could expound at length about the notion of sufficiency in scientific theory), explained that it was the heat of his palms that turned the mercury to frenzied bubbling and made the capsule bounce and teeter as if there were a drunken wcrm in it.

Two days later he produced a refined version with the capsule painted pretty like an Easter egg. He showed it to his compadre, Chalo, who knew a jobber in El Paso. ¡Qué amigazo! They went to see the jobber. The jobber went to see a plastics manufacturer, a man with great metal presses and centrifuges to force molten plastic into little cavities.

There were endless delays, boredom, abulia. My father quickly got fed up with waiting and decided to invent something else. He put together a plastic submarine out of a Revell box, bored two holes in it and filled them with hoses. He pumped air in and out with a hand pump. The sub went up and down "like magic." With the other pump he fired a dart-like torpedo out of the submarine's hulk. The ship was not a total success. A little rough water in the bathtub and the sub would roll over like a dead bull-head on the Río Grande. "It's the balance," my dad said. "The balance has to be perfect. The tolerances are too fine. After all, plastic weighs nothing. You'd have to be a real engineer to solve it."

My father didn't consider himself a "real" engineer. He was smart enough to know that he was some sort of claptrap genius and also to know that he had no credentials. Maybe he considered himself on a par with a "jailhouse" lawyer. He used the adjective "real" like a scourge and a vision.

About six months later we spotted my baby sister, Conchita, playing with one of those merry, lifeless beans. My dad turned from his domino game and glared at her, with malevolence. "Where'd you get that!"

Conchita began to quiver. "I traded it at school for two clear marbles!"

"They have them at school!"

"Yes."

"Everybody has them?"

Conchita nodded.

And so it was finished with the automatic jumping beans. Except for the malestar that it left in my father's gut. He didn't really care about the royalties that he had fantasized over. He just wished more people knew who the real inventor was. We never talked or told anyone else about it. We made ourselves forget.

That was one thing I couldn't tolerate about my father. We were witness to a succession of unprincipled ruses that were played upon my father's person to the discredit of the family honor. Part of it was that fatalism characteristic of Papi's generation, that passive resignation and acceptance of "reality." That was difficult to stomach, yet certainly not unique; it was the norm, therefore tolerable. To this my father added a boundless and totally unfounded faith in people. He was an ingenue, a trusting child, a father to all his charges. And what's more, men, including confidence men, had confidence in him.

How my old man had faith! And he'd been in and out of so many operations. He had scoured the Southwest for old batteries to haul across the border to transform into lead ingots and sell back to the Americans; he had stamped out Jesus Christs on metal plate, struck Virgin Marys from rubber molds, learned the ins and outs of libraries in order to invent a process to detin cans; he had set diamonds, manufactured brass buttons for the armed forces, designed costume jewelry, set up a nickel-plating bath, run a route of gumball machines, managed a molino de nixtamal for tortillas, bought a chicken farm (without having read Sherwood Anderson), gone to school at the Polytechnic, bred rabbits, trained geese to be industrial watchdogs, raised a family and invented the automatic jumping bean. He trained scores of young men in the techniques of lathes, presses, files and baths. He was able to initiate not a few followers into the mysteries of the electro-mechanical creed. But after his accident with the sodium hydroxide he shut himself in. Now and then one of his former disciples would come over with a sixpack to pay his respects. These men would be foremen at the mine at Smeltertown or supervisors of the toaster assembly line at the Magic Chef complex. Papi was pleased with his pupils but he used them as case studies—fox and crow style—to prove his point that my brother and I had to get college degrees as engineers. "There's no other way," my dad told us continually. "You have to have a passport."

In some circles my father was considered a soft touch. The chicken farm went broke after my father hired an holgazán with no experience "y unos huevos de plomo." A year after he convinced el patrón to get into the detinning business, everybody was privy and there were eight detinners in Juárez alone. Besides, they started coming out with the aluminum can. The geese functioned beautifully but he couldn't convince enough people to accept the idea. The War was over and nobody needed brass buttons. After a while his eyesight wasn't so good and he couldn't set diamonds. The big companies didn't like the idea of him moving into religious jewelry, so they muscled him out at the retail level. The United States customs officials raised the tariff on lead ingots. The gumballs got all sticky inside their machines in the Juárez sun. Somebody invented the automatic tortilla press and nobody needed raw corn dough. He never was able to graduate from the Polytechnic—after eight years of going at night he was doing an isometric drawing of a screw and he stopped and said he wouldn't. We ate lots of rabbit and someone went ahead and manufactured automatic jumping beans without informing my father.

I spent five years in college; for three of those I tried to be an engineer. Go be an engineer! Get thee to an engine! My father would pin my shoulders to the wall and lecture me with manic glee. Me and my younger brother would not only be engineers—but metallurgists! He feared for his poor Mexico-Americanized sons, alloys of detinned beer cans. Appreciable schizophrenes. Unable to speak a tongue of any convention, they gabbled to each other, the younger and the older, in a papiamento of street caliche and devious calques. A tongue only Tex-Mexs, wetbacks, tirilones, pachucos and pochos could penetrate. Heat the capsule in the palm of your hand and the mercury begins seesawing and the capsule hops. Those were his sons, transplanted, technocratic, capsular Mexican jumping beans without the worm. He believed in education and a free press. Would society listen to reason?

My father liked to walk in the barrio and as hijo mayor it was my privilege to be at his side. We'd walk down the main drag, past the chicharronería ("sin pelos, ¿eh?") where the pork rind hung to dry, and past the molino de nixtamal where at six in the morning you could queue up for the masa that came out like sausage from the funnel and was molded into a ball and sold like a pumpkin on a scale. Invariably we'd look at what was doing at the movies but we never went in. It would be either a Mexican flick like *Ustedes los ricos* or *Nosotros los pobres* with Pedro Infante or Jorge Negrete, or a World War II gringada with Spanish subtitles. John Garfield scowling like a Protestant moralist with a tommy gun emerging from his vientre. We would wind up at my father's favorite tortería, El Mandamás del Barrio. My dad would have a short beer and I'd wolf down some nieve de mamey. Then followed a half-hour rap between Papi and the braggadocio owner, don Ernesto. They would share their mutual entrepreneurial visions. Going home my father could become very moody. He would compart his frustrations and his hopes. He made me feel like a true varón and I would listen to and guard his words jealously and, from the time I was twelve, with intense anguish. My father usually couched his ambitions in terms of money or some other material objective (dólares vs. dolores). But it was transparent even to a youngster that his true goals were more intangible. He spoke of handing down an inheritance or heritage to his sons, a patrimony, a family business, the establishment of a new order. This pleased me. What I feared was his attribution of responsibility. His resentments had become self-directed; he blamed himself for his failures, he knew he was a brilliant man and yet, somehow, his objectivity about the physical world had become perversely countervailed by a totally immoderate estimation of his position in it. Perhaps it was his pride and hunger for recognition that accounted for his overweening hunger for blame. Even his accident at the detinning plant he figured, along with the insurance companies, as some "act of God." My father had no sense of being suppressed; he believed in his freedom of action to a degree that, at the age of twelve, imbued me with fearful trembling for my own personal accountability. He pressed his sons hard on the school issue. School didn't matter to him particularly as a medium of factual knowledge (much less wisdom); he pushed it on us as a means of attaining the necessary credentials—un pasaporte was the term he used with blind naiveté for the connotations of his choice. School, or rather, graduation and the diploma were a passport into America. It permitted the bearer to travel the road royal.

One evening, as usual, my father was questioning me with meticulous detail about my schoolwork. I told him that tomorrow I would have to crucify a frog. It was for junior high biology and sad and dreadful. For two weeks Maestro Rodríguez, a maestro fiercely loved by me, had been methodically outlining with a piece of yellow chalk on a slate board the life mechanisms of the green frog. I had committed the life to memory, consuming him organ by organ. Tomorrow I was to force him open. After the frog was dunked in anesthesia I was to nail him to a piece of plywood. That was the crucifixion part, his little limbs completely distended so that the torso would be exposed to the public, scientific eye. A disturbing image which my father relished; a frog pinned like a man or boy with arms and legs stretched out on the edges of a raft, belly up on the infinite green sea . . . And then I would use the stainless steel razor to cut the frog into twin symmetries. I was to remove and label the liver, the heart, the brain. I was required to identify the optic nerve.

That evening my father had more than one short beer at El Mandamás del Barrio and I had more than one nieve in order to sweeten my mouth. We were troubled and enchanted by the imagery of pollywog martyrdom. When we went home my father was more moody than usual. He looked like a sullen, pathetic victim. The honor in his jaw had softened and he almost seemed to be pouting. He transmitted to me an uncontrollable trembling and a fear for my life and integrity. The most dreadful thing was that none of it could hinder me or make a difference. In the morning I would put on my blue school uniform and go to my biology class and do what I must do.

One day in college when I was staggering around the stacks and fell across Jung's Psychology and Alchemy, I had an inkling of what my papi's metallurgy was all about. Alchemy: The transformation of dross into gold and the fashioning of the gold into a higher, purer meaning. The goose that laid the golden egg. Out of your ass, man! I spent three years in college dunning the physical world for a sense of reality. I learned all about the acids, bases and salts. They took on a moral connotation for me. But I never could get much realization from the natural world. I preferred reading a novel or loving a woman. At that time my father was semi-retirado. His face had been disfigured by a geyser of caustic soda when the detinning bath blew. For over six months something had been going awry with the bath. Every three or four weeks there would be this awful rumbling and out of the tank ten feet long by ten feet wide would spout a geyser of boiling caustic soda and tin slush. My father was very concerned. The workers were coming on the job with heavy rubber tarpaulins close at hand. There was muttering that this was hazardous work and they should get a raise. My dad walked around with a yellow pad; he kept scribbling numbers. Every day he dropped his plumb-line into the foul-smelling tank and took a reading of the solution level. He was convinced that the variation in the buildup of incrustation at the bottom of the tank had led to substantial variations in temperature within the solution. When the temperature differences became too extreme: the geyser effect. He advised that the tank be drained and that the incrustations be scraped from the bottom so that the solution would receive uniform heat. But el patrón wouldn't hear of it. There was too fierce a competition for the scarce tin cans. If they were out of business for two, three weeks, they'd never get back on beam. What they had to do was plumb the tank for all it was worth and when she blew, ¡que se joda! If necessary they would go back to old batteries and lead ingots. One day my father was standing over the tank with his plumbline. He looked like a little bronze boy fishing in a vat of vaporous split-pea soup. Suddenly, without warning, the physical world spat up at him. He took a sop of alkaline base right on the head. Very funny! Just like Laurel and Hardy. What the hell, there's only a finite number of tin cans anyway. Besides, my dad would never have to worry anymore that he was being discriminated against merely because he was Hispanic.

After the accident Papi mostly stayed at home, although he was known to beat it out occasionally to Chalo's for un partidito de dominó. He gave up his vocation as a subpatrón, a teacher,

trainer and overseer of men. He claimed he wasn't up to breaking in new men with his face disfigured as it was. He wouldn't be
able to face the chisme and derision of resentful ingenues. He
had taken it on himself and it made him lose his confidence. Now
and then he'd get an inspiration and rush to his closet, which he
had fashioned into a shop, and work over a virgin hunk of metal
with his press and files.

Chalito and I went to college, where after many peripeteias I
eventually majored in sociology. In the afternoon my brother and
I ran the gumball route for el patrón. In our pickup we wandered
through all the good and bad-ass neighborhoods of El Paso and
Ciudad Juárez. Everywhere we stopped a horde of expectant
esquintles descended on us. "¡Ahí vienen los chicleros! Dame un
chicle, ¿no?"

My old man made it easier for the gumball business when he
invented some kind of corn oil to spray on the gumballs so they
wouldn't stick to the glass or to each other. On the other hand,
it was our solemn duty to fix the charms to the glass sides of
the machine so they couldn't fall down the gum slot and requite
some grimy-pawed tot in his vision of hitting the gordo from a
magnanimous vending machine. My dad even discovered that it
was easier to give the storeowner's 15% cut of the sales by weight
rather than having to count out all the money. Some storeowners
were not so certain, however, about the reliability of mass in
the physical world and they needed constant convincing that
weight and count were equivalent. Every once in a while they'd
"keep us honest" by making us count the money too.

It was a tolerable life and when I graduated from college my
father was present in his dark blue suit and dark tie (the combo
he reserved for a funeral), feeling proud and tender and somewhat ill at ease about his scarred, reprehensible face. He poured
me a tequila with his own hand and made me lick the salt from
his own wrist. "You've made something of yourself!" he told me.
He was not too sure about the nature of these "social" sciences
but he was confident that the degree would satisfy the contin-
gencies of the "real" world. When he died, perhaps from boredom, loneliness and a thwarted imagination, he laid a heavy rap
on me. He said I was the oldest and therefore I inherited the
responsibilities. I should see to it that the family was kept intact,

go about the unfinished business of establishing some solid, familiar enterprise, a patrimony.

If I did not forgive my father his naive belief in his omnipotence then I would have succumbed to his logic and in condemning him would validate his credo of an ultimate, personal accountability. The vicious circle; the double bind. It is better to forgive him and lay the blame on a myopic, racist society that would have granted a white Anglo of his talents an adequate station in life. This position too has its fearful hazards for it alienates me from my father's vision and his wishes. Pater noster. His love for and exuberant response to the world pose a momentous challenge. His younger son made it as an engineer. He works for General Dynamics where he helps design submarines.

He was a man who inspired confidence . . . I prefer to fix him as he was when I was twelve. It was long before the vat full of sodium hydroxide had turned eccentric and he was at his height of virility and joy. One golden afternoon after school I went down to the detinning plant and peered through the fence at the scrap metal yard. The yard was one square kilometer wide and filled to the brim with brilliant metal. It was a splendid day and my father had decided to do some physical work with his men. He sported a magnificent Zapatista mustache. He had taken off his shirt and his bronze chest and arms rippled with muscles as he dug into a mound eight feet high of shimmering scrap and filled a massive wire cage. He looked like bronze Neptune with his trident or maybe like a revolutionary poster of an industrial worker emanating joyous aggression. The workers were laughing and marveling as he filled the wire cage in six minutes and then attached it to the crane that hauled it to the tank of caustic soda. I wanted to go inside the yard but I was fearful because Papi's trained geese honked militantly at me from the other side of the fence. At that time I was about the same height as these ferocious bull geese and a week earlier one had pecked me on the cheek. Neither the bruise nor the moral outrage had healed. Finally the geese became distracted by a stray dog and I made a dash for it. My father greeted me with delight as if I were a creature unique, a novelty. We went to the furnace where they melted the batteries. He knew the furnace fascinated me. He let some of the molten lead down the channel and into the ingot molds. Molten lead does not look base at all but rather like fine Spanish silver. We inspected the artisans who fashioned the soles for huaraches out of old rubber tires. We checked out the rabbits who also lived in the yard. There was a white fluffy one I enjoyed petting and laying on certain prepubertal fantasies.

During the break the young macho workers would place a narrow board ten feet long by ten feet wide across the steaming and bubbling vat of caustic soda. The brackish vat looked like a place on Venus where Flash Gordon might land and the machos liked to reassure themselves by walking over the board they had laid across the corrosive brew. My father did not approve of this practice. As a man of responsibility and devout observer of the physical world he believed to the utmost in the principles of safety. Unfortunately the young workers did not share his sense of caution and they played their little game. That day they invited a brand-new worker to walk his way across the board, just in order to verify his machismo. This worker did so without the slightest hesitation. He walked across once and was rewarded with the promise of a free beer. He walked over again and received another free beer. He was supremely confident. He went over again and stumbled into the vat. The worker had heavy rubber boots but before he could catch his balance he went in over the knee and the solution filled up his boot. The workers were hollering and my father came running with a fire extinguisher filled with neutralizer. They got the worker's boot off and a patch of skin from the man's calf came peeling off with the boot. My father foamed what was left of the leg and wrapped a blanket around it.

The ambulance seemed to never come. For me and perhaps for others present the young worker had somehow been transformed and transported to an inhuman category. He was no longer like me, he was something alien, revolting and mortifying, something with which I could no longer identify. But my father held him in his arms and comforted him. The young worker was in such intense pain and shock that he could not scream. He whispered to my father if he would be short a leg. My father was too committed a realist to deny it. He clenched the young man's hand in his own. He talked to the worker about the dignity of work. He told the worker that the leg didn't matter, that maybe he wasn't el patrón but he was el subpatrón and after he was well he would see to it that there was work for him.

My question is: Why wasn't Papi recognized as the inventor of the wormless bean and other joyous novelties?

The Mojado Who Offered Up His Tapeworms to the Public Weal

¡Oyez, oyez! ease your wearies and you shall learn about the case of the State versus the hapless, peripatetic mojao, a surely woeful account in the main—a sucker mojao who slipped across the Bravo stepping stones in a snorkel, flippers, and a toy-store trident—but not without socially redeeming values as well as intimations of brave third worlds, indeed a tale with certain exuberant dimensions of H. Alger-like mobility to which all we citizens of this good nation still (or ought still) respond.

First let me alert you to my editorial intentions. This account as first told to me meandered worse than the Río Grande itself and I mean to edit it. Moreover, I shall want to focus on the moment of conversion, with its sepia qualities of the old print or Far West photo, of the pícaro who once he is scourged and brought to escarmiento (that of course is the moment when our mojao offers up his tapeworms to the public weal) takes to clean living and his place as a far-seeing subject of the State. And it's a totally true story too, I heard it firsthand from a gentlemen—digo un gentilhombre—known as one el Rompeculos, in the Trailways station in Earth, Texas. We were casual fellow travelers killing our drudgery as we languished in Earth waiting for the express to come in and take us straight to Ajo, Arizona, and then to San Diego (San Dedo to those who know it well) with blessedly brief pit (piss) stops in Muleshoe, Needmore, Bronco, Humble City, Jal, Wink, Pecos, Boracho, Eagle Flat, Tornillo, Socorro, Chamberino, Bawtry, Bowie, Cochise, Mescal, Pan Tak, Suwuki Chuapo, Quijotoa, Tracy, and Why. Among the ceaseless hours of waiting and the Chili Dogs, wet and dry burritos, and the juicy jujubes, we took to snorting, piston-like, shots of translucent Pancho Villa tequila (haven't you tried that brand? It's sold ex-

clusively in liquor stores across from bus stations and strictly in
$1.99 units), alternating them with swallows of homemade terra-
cotta-colored border-town sangrita which one of my companion's
amigas had brew-mistressed, tempered with chile pequín, and
measured out for Rompe in an ornate onyx flagon.

"Why do they call you Huitlacoche?"

"I choose to call myself that."

"I know it as something to eat. A mushroom or fungus that
grows on corn."

"I know him as a boxer I admired some years ago who being
a poor Indian became wealthy with his fists and returned wealth
to the poor."

"Oh, him. I remember him. Didn't he once fight in the Mexico
City bullring?"

"Yes."

"Good."

"Why do they call you Rompeculos?"

"I choose to call myself that. Basically because I'm an arrogant
chop buster."

"Good."

This Rompeculos, a muscular brute perhaps about 40 years
old with a tattoo of the Aztlanense eagle gorging itself on la ser-
piente, who as my narration will definitely prove had the gentle,
inquisitive sensibility of a schizoid poet, was a sometime hauler
of Coors beer along the desert floors and byways. Contrary to
what the inside covers of matchbooks so gamely enthuse for
ingenues, he really had learned to master the big rigs, and was
used to making significant bread—when he worked at this handle—hauling 6000 cases of Coors in a 14 wheel semi and an extra
8 wheeler in tow. He was, of course, a sometime contrabandist,
this being the borderland, after all. As for trucking though, as he
put it, the "blow job" could get to you. He'd be driving down the
Waco run and in the dead night of desert air, all by his lonely, with
only a pinup of Sylvia Pinal or María Dolores or Flor Silvestre
above his shield to keep him company—Dios es mi copiloto—
when suddenly one of those 99 bottles way in back would blow.
That's it. They would have been all shook up by their tripping and
suddenly he'd hear one blow and a few minutes later another
would pop its cap and gush forth and five big ones down the road
it would be a third coming to climax. I guessed then that the beer,

that was his problem. But I was mistaken. At any rate, here he was, a little down and out in Earth, Texas, precisely where I was.

"What'cha here for, hombre?"

"Well, I needed some chavos to continue my studies at the uni."

He looked at me cross-eyed, like el pícaro that he was. "You a college kid?"

I got very sullen. Being a brutish sight myself, and a higher education gridironist, I felt an occasional prerogative to be temperamental. "I'm not a kid. I'm back from Nam."

" 'Ta bien. What do you play, middle linebacker? You're huge enough. You here on a bandit run?"

"Something like that. ¡Pero de mala muerte!"

"They fucked you over, ése?"

"Yeah, man. I was supposed to score enough Irapuato green to get me through my junior year. I came down all the way to the central altiplano y pues nada, puro pedo."

"Shit, man. En Irapuato, puras fresas. Ese, that's all they sell there, strawberries. And even be careful with those man, cause the top berries look real good and plump como los besos de una vieja salada but down below they're all huangas and overripe. No, ése, to Irapuato for fresas and to Morelia for morelianas and to Guanajuato, de tan alta alcurnia, for camotes (camo te vienes, camo te vas, camote te meto por detrás—they don't call me Rompeculos for nothing), and to Veracruz for huachinangos, not to mention huapangos, and to Aguascalientes for the best goddamned cockfights you ever saw in your whole life, digo, la feria. But for mota, man, you've got to get way up high, see? Up in the foothills around Toluca, up in the mountains by Amecameca where you can see prince Popo copulating with princess Ixta. Up high, ése, that's where the mota is, Toluca green."

"Oye vato, thanks so much for telling me this shit now that it can do me no good. Aquí pues estoy en mero rasquachi eating pecan chunkies on the bench in Earth, Texas."

"Aw, don't worry about it, ése. Supposing you did score, then you would have had to move your stash across the border. A tenderfoot college vato like you. Who knows what might have happened. You could have ended up like that jerk in the movies, the Midnight Express. It can happen. I'm telling you cause I know." Rompe scratched his head and squinted. "Let me give you some advice, Huitla. Forget about the foliage, it's pure risk man, especially if you're not enchufado into a border brokerage. Next time you come down, run a few parrots. Más vale."

"Parrots? ¿'Tas loco?"

"I'm telling you, man. Pound for pound they'll make more money for you than marihuana. You can buy parrots on the streets of Laredo for maybe 25 or 30 dollars. You know what they go for in San Antonio? Three hundred big ones! A little further inland, say Kansas City, seven hundred, no más. And with a parrot you've got fluidity. You take your investment to any good pet shop y ahí no más, they exchange it for currency, just like at the bank."

"I don't know, vato loco. I wouldn't buy no parrot but for sure I'd buy a lid of mota."

"That's because you don't know birds, ése. They're the only ones that will accept a human. You can raise a pigeon and it'll do acrobatics but you can't get one to crawl on your finger or hop on your head. The parrot alone will tolerate human companionship. People love them because they become like humans. You teach them to talk, to sing. They've got perfect pitch. I've got one myself. It sings strictly songs of the Mexican Revolution. You know, *Adelita, La Valentina, el 30-30.*"

Finally the Trailways bus arrived. Feeling very tipsy we lurched our way to the Earth men's room to empty our bladders. Then we boarded the bus, picking seats up front where it was less bumpy.

Rompe continued his sermonizing. "All you do is douse their bread with a little tequila and take them over the bridge in a sack under your seat or donde sea. And if you get caught, ¿qué importa? At most a fifty dollar fine, if they even bother. Cause nobody takes parrots seriously, not even the customs agents. With marihuana they can catch up with you 500 miles north of the border. But pericos! ¡Qué ricos! Once they're across you can't prove a damned thing!"

"You're making me sad, Rompe. Real sad. You know how I'm going to spend this summer? Breading shrimp at Arthur Treacher's or grating that foul cheese they use at Taco Bell. Puta madre, and the worst was that my cucaracha conked out in the sierras. It did, it slipped a rod and I had no lana to get it mended."

"So what you do man, you junk it? What's the matter, don't you guys get a football scholarship?"

"Yeah, they throw us a bone, but college is expensive, especially for a Chicano b.m.o.c."

Rompe shrugged his head. "So where's your cucaracha?"

"What could I do, they wouldn't even buy it, a car with U.S. plates in Mexico. Finally some wool brokers in Chihuahua city gave me some lana for it, mostly for the radio although they claimed que tenían modo de arreglar lo de las placas."

Rompe laughed. "I know that Chihuahua wool-gathering crowd, they're enchufadísimo con la aduana. For sure they must've cleared five hundred, maybe a grand on your fotingo. What year was it? What model?"

I just looked at him aggrieved and drank maybe two fingers worth of tequila.

Rompe looked me over as if for the first time, con sospechas y cautela. "You studying to be a doctor?"

"¡Esos! I hate those fuckers."

"¿Pues qué?"

"Poet. ¡Pueta! A nomad."

"¿Poeta? What kind of career is that? You're a strange guy, Huitla. And your name is as strange as you. ¿Qué tú haces? You eat magic mushrooms? ¡Hay que vender la mota y no esfumarla!" He had a big poet's belly laugh, a shot of Pancho Villa's best and a good swallow of fiery sangrita, settled back into his pullman seat and told me this tale about a woeful friend of his: un mojao.

Now, this story meandered up and down into every backwater and eddy like the Río Bravo itself. I mean, please don't think that I'm going to bore you with the sort of river flotsam he laid on me—the bit about how this mojao once managed a molino de nixtamal, overseeing the mixing of the corn with water and slaked lime in order to produce the gruel that would then be ground into masa harina while the benditas queued up at 6:00 a.m. for their supplies, or how he landed an RFP from the Yuma, Arizona, CETA to offer a crash course to ex-junkies on how to train geese to be industrial watchdogs for the junkyard business (meaner than junkyard dogs! was the program's motto), or how during one period he painted watercolors of cherubs, madonnas and 31 types of chirping birdies on birch barks for los turistas, or how he seduced the wife of el mero chingón jefe de la Falfurrias migra, or the sweatshop he labored in that produced synthetic blue pellets supposed to look like genuine turquoise in order to imitate the jewelry of the Santo Domingo Pueblos, or all those other border conceits. No, none of that, but I must declare, some of this pueta's story—it was like you are panning the Río Bravo for precious substance and all you come up with on your plate is dead catfish after toxic catfish and suddenly there's this clunker, the fabled nugget that made the Golden West—well now, that is something to polish and assay. So, Dios mediante, I would like now to focus on this meandering mojado and that golden moment when he redeemed himself in the eyes of his Anglo overseers through the ordained intercession of the therapeutic tapeworms that thrived in his infected bowels. Let us make a beginning y ahí va de cuento.

Erase un mojado pero muy mojao. According to his cuate el Rompeculos, who knew this wet from the very start and, it could be claimed, dogged him at key intervals like the cartoon angel of good conscience, he was born in the massive wheatfields of Sinaloa, labored in those fields with all-told thirteen brethren (and sistern?) reaping the wheat from wither our daily tortillas are patted and fashioned to fill our panzas with cheese and bean burritos. Nothing out of the ordinary, this young, rude, clever, robust, and fearfully ignorant country chamacón, living his days and laboring mightily in the breadbasket of northwestern Mexico, a plains mozalbete who knew no further than Guamuchil to the west and Mocorito to the east. This life was—how can I convey to you the idyll of laborious ignorance?—the bliss of unremitting and unselfconscious routines, an agrarian, Skinnerian utopia (as Keats put it, to think is to be filled with sorrow), until one day, it was about puberty or maybe a bit into it already, he found himself returning the coa to the long white stable of the latifundio and came upon his two older sisters lying on their backs in the straw with their skirts up and their comely legs spread, each with a handsome caballerango on top doing a flopping dance like contrincantes in a cockfight or partners in a horizontal jarabe. Steadfastly he shut the door on the intrusion into his vida. Pero, ¡ay maldito! ya se le entraba el gusanito de las dudas. A dirt road traveling true through the wheatfields was no longer merely a dirt road but a segmented trajectory over time. It was a vector with a retrospect and a prospective future. The signals of nuestra vida natural suddenly took on a new semiotic. What was that arboreal warble that correlated with a young peon's erection? and that long fastidious mutter of oxen that harmonized with a mancebo's inchoate brooding, and finally, passionate resentments? As Rompe judged it, in that establo parpadeo our young mojao had eaten of nuestra manzana del saber and ultimately—as every mojao must feel so deeply in order to be mojao, that is, genuinely driven into border waters—tasted the notion of class.

One day our mojao was musing and chewing his emotional cud by the fire in his adobe home. The firelight made a suppurative dance on the caked wall and ultimately on the breast of his younger sister Consuelo, and for the first time our pre- and proto-mojado looked upon his sister and himself with foreknowledge. There was young Consuelo, whose breasts rose like certain rivers in times of flood—a natural and irreversible consequence of the springtime or of puberty; poor Consuelo, suddenly and without warning tears streaming down her golden firelit cheeks, her rising, yearning, uncontrollable pechos.

And our mojado knew direction. A triptych the first panel of which put in place the prior conducta of his two older sisters, those very traitors to rural vida who long since had departed flamboyantly on the backs of potros negros, the made mates of mustachioed caballerangos, the kind of varones machos that the Sinaloan wheatfields so proudly boost and supply with field machetes of tempered steel. No longer would his vida contain within it the dulcet periodicity of the three nights a year, el Día de los Muertos, la Nochebuena, el Domingo de Gloria, when these loving archangels would with infinite care fashion festive tamales and fill them with ground walnuts, with coconut, pineapple or strawberries, and feed him, madonna fingers to chamaco mouth. They had been carried away by the implacable, migratory wind and he knew in that moment that he would never see them again.

In the second retable he saw Consuelo, who grew to beauty by days, by discrete moments before the fire that lit adobe walls and the slanted morning sun that illuminated swaying, bread-bearing grasses. Growing to beauty her pechos swelled hopelessly, advertising themselves against her will. She suffered and he suffered with her the bodily rackings of pubertal premonitions, the foreknowledge (and the foreskin) of carnal perdición. He

knew this, saw it transmitted from his meaning-laden gaze to the
eyes of his dear unsuccored sister, her campesina's eyes, so
unused to manifested extremes of feeling, now clouding before
revealed truths, a break in the stoic line of her lips. Finally a peasant's sigh issued from inside Consuelo, a sigh patterned on those
she had heard from time to time emitted by peasant women who
sit in visitation of their loved ones in the camposanto.

And el viejo saw this too, "viejo vivo," chuckled Rompe as he
recounted this all on a bus that opened up on the Earth to Ajo
trailway like a farting jogger in the clear—"porque más sabe el
diablo por viejo que por diablo."

"Yes," said Rompe, who gave high marks—a poet's premium—
to those who know even though they cannot act upon what they
know. "Los que saben, saben, the viejo just looked up from where
he was resting, rose to his haunches on his petate, looked at his
son, el mojao sin todavía serlo, with a knowing, señorial air, and
then at Consuelo and her heaving, autonomous breasts and said,
'¡Ay Consuelo! Parece que tú vas a ser el Consuelo de los hombres.' "

And then, as if this axiological and ontogenetic proposition
had been mustered at great physical expense, el viejo crouched
back into the adobe shadow, only his eyes visible as brooding
points.

And our pobre mojado looked first at his inconsolable sister,
for whom the mandates of rural honor and vergüenza would
dictate the most vigorous sibling defense of her virginal status,
and then at his father, pater noster, nuestro señor de todos los
mojados, a man who had conceived and raised a robust and
nutrido prole, who had always operated within the narrow ortho-
doxies of the code of the countryside; now only his eyes were
still driven, some message for our mojado in them surely of laissez
faire, a blessing of mobility (outward if not upward) from our
father of the wetbacks, our viejo who had been a proverbial Sinaloan template of a villano en su rincón but for whom no Lope sang
paeans of rustic praise, no Fuenteovejuna had risen in defense, no
reasoned alcalde had intervened against mustachioed machos
and their brandished machetes, no Zapata had offered land much
less liberty, no Villa, no Orozco, no Obregón had risen a dedo
meñique much less offered an arm, not even a Demetrio Macías
to offer a fatalistic appreciation of the inertia (punctuated by

staccato and unavoidable all-be-them clearly heralded catastrophes) of his wheatfield peonage.

Now to the third retable, himself down low, his member perniciously rising like a volcanic promontory—¡un Paricutín!—from the humdrum llano, an icon erect in the latifundio, feeding itself on the sorrowful solace of autonomous breasts and the acquiescent despair of worn-out lives, generating libido, as must be the case of any mojao who is truly a mojao, from motives that give impetus to the transgression of taboos. Our mojado knew then in that moment by the shrinking fire of his peon's hearth, in his own swelling, robust sex that was foremost (and foreskin) an act of wet defiance to the social and filial orders, that he would be departed in the morning, onto the dirt road that would become a dusty tar ribbon to Juárez (city in turn founded in the name of a mighty rural leader and iconoclast), there to mingle with a veritable ragtag army of wets recruited from the countless villages, hamlets, and milpas of the sovereign interior of México. This was Juárez before the maquiladoras and the pleasing rhetoric of the Chamizal, where certain women were paid pesos or dollars to do dirty deeds with donkeys.

As I sorted out this torrent of words which gushed forward from el Rompeculos and doubled back into prefixed rhetorical rivulets, I was at once caught in the web of this hip and coarse narrator, and tugged by a certain anxiety. This man did not fit clearly into the slot or stereotype that I had fashioned for him.

"Did you go to college?"

"Hell no! ¿Y por qué lo preguntas?"

"I don't know. You seem so awfully knowledgeable. Are you claiming that your mojado friend left home because he was aroused by his sister? What am I supposed to think? That he became errant to maintain the fiction, or perchance more poignantly, the reality of his sister's chaste honor? Or what?"

Rompe chuckled. "Don't exaggerate, poeta. On the other hand a mojado must cross waters to be truly one, isn't that so? And don't ask me again about college. ¡Qué college ni que college! I am a citizen, and a leading one, I might add, of the Third World. Try to understand that. You come down to our world looking for some pin money to carry you through a semester—¿y qué? This is not México. This is not the United States. This is a third land, a band or contraband 2000 miles long and 200 miles wide. It runs from the sand dunes of Matamoros to the seacliffs of La Jolla. It's run by its own logic and psychologic; it cooks up its own Tex-Mex food, concocts a language called pocho, musters its own police, la migra. Its felons are sui generis. Where else can a guy get busted for running double yellowheaded parrots, dealing in transnational lobster and shrimp or smuggling flasks of mercury and truckloads of candelilla? Its city-states hang on each side of the frontier, tit for tat, Tecate and Tecate, Calexico and Mexicali, San Luis and San Luis, Gringo Pass and Sonoyta, Sasabe and Sásabe, Nogales and Nogales, Naco and Naco, Columbus and Palomas, Laredo and Nuevo Laredo, Progreso and Nuevo Progreso, like brother and sister—forgive this somewhat Malinchesque although not unjustified analogy—copulating in the night with one eye over their shoulders making sure that faraway parents are not spying.

"While it may pay tribute to remote power centers—Washington, Distrito Federal and other humbug—this borderland, which I will now christen on this pathetic Earth to Ajo express as Mexérica, functions like a satrapy. No borderline here but a wriggling membrane that soaks in produce and spits out product. Its city-states own themselves and are committed almost totally to their own introspective, autistic symbiosis—more appropriately to the relationship of the shark and the pilot fish, the yucca plant and the yucca moth, or the commensalism of the beneficent tapeworms and their human host.

"And the currency. That is what is most peculiarly wet. More than the transnationalism or the transgressions, it's the transactions. As a country we are most like a Wall Street, a brokerage. Power seekers, power brokers, and the impotent; all cross this river, where there is a river. We have dealers in orifices, in euphoria, in human futures and orange juice futures, in man's labor, in the fruit of women's labor, in Christmas tree ornaments, silicon chips and semiconductors, and toothpaste. A friend of mine is the biggest 'importer' into Mexico of fiberglass drapes. This is a world that makes a market in sadists and masochists, in siervos and señores, in capitalists and wild-eyed revolutionaries . . ."

"And vatos locos too, right ése? Wild-eyed poets, exuberant truck drivers?"

"Yes, Mr. Huitlacoche, them too, as well as b.m.o.c. Chicanos. Do you know how far we have branched out? Do you know how much certain labor-intensive industries depend on us? I'm not talking about hotels, mister. I mean steel and petrochemicals! Do you know how much San Antonio depends on us; hell, do you know how Chicago depends on us? We are branching out mister, we've opened up consulates or dealerships—en esta tierra son la misma cosa—in El Salvador, Nicaragua, Bolivia, Colombia, Perú, you name it, if it's impoverished and still retains some minimal level of aspiration, we've got a presence. Hell, I could show you a store on Laredo's Convent Street. A modest, unimposing grocery, where they sell more Tide, Pet Milk and Kool-Aid than anyplace else on this earth. When I read about the developing world, the Third World with its massive infusions of people and currencies, its Aswan dams, its World Banks, I am amused. This is a Third World. Dollars are changed into pesos, pesos to dollars, it is a barterworld and a borderworld, the only frontier on earth where the truly poor commingle with the well-to-do inhabitants of the richest, most spoiled nation on earth. This band, this contraband, my nation Mexérica, Amexica, is a fulsome place of economic growth. It is also a cloaca into which drains the commingled phantasmagoria of the richest and the poorest. And I am one of its citizens and self-adumbrated bards." Our rompeculos of the mojados then chortled, downed another two fingers of Pancho Villa and slumped into his seat.

We had been on the express for over six hours and it was a very dark vehicle that sped us to the first reaches of New Mexico. Most of our fellow crew slept fitfully. Here and there one could detect buzzing patches of conversation.

"Tell me then, Rompe, what happened to our young mojao when he reached the wicked city?"

Rompe yawned. "Nothing special. He didn't stay young too long. He learned. He became borderwise and shed his fieldish ways for fiendish ones. From what he told me I figure he was a mite stupider than most. One huckster convinced him to run the river on his own. This poor stupid mojao had saved maybe 60 to 70 bucks as a result of long hours of toil painting little angels and doves on almate bark for the gabacho tourists, and he threw his lana to the coyote who donned him up with a snorkel, flippers, a diving mask, and to add irony to injury, a little trident made of plastic that mocked King Neptune's sovereignty. Then he gave him a copy of one of those 'secret maps' that abound in the Golden West, pointing to everything from treasure to choice bends in the river, and set him off to swim the Río Grande. Except that in that place and at that time of the year the water was so low that he lost his huarache—I mean his flipper—across the stepping stones in the water. Here our mojao was, in the dead of night, dressed up in his sporting-goods store best, slipping over the dead bullheads beached on the riverbed stones. And all the time the officers of la migra are waiting in their cop car, trying so hard to muffle their laughter that they're shitting. You see, it was all a set-up. A cruel practical joke. When wettie gets over to the other side they flash a beam on him and fall down in mirth. One by one the officers go to relieve themselves by the river. Then they apprehend their delincuente, fleece him of his garb and throw him back across the border. When el mojao gets back to the cantina all his acquaintances are clued in."

"Hey hombres, here comes el indito!"

"The one who dressed up like the Creature from the Black Lagoon!"

"He just got back from el coloso del norte!"

"What's the matter, Macario? You look all wet!"

"Oye, indio triste, lend me some money from what you made pizcando melones!"

The "Mojado According to Rompe" follows a different story line from there, and then it turns again and takes a third direction. What seems to be clear though is that this ése of rural honor, perhaps partially because of the warped joke, turned to re-enacting the role of mojado, emerging baptismally from the Río Bravo time and time again. For one, although he was as clever and adroit as any, he refused to learn much of the English language. Moreover, basing himself on the Mexican side of the river he sought out opportunities that required continual round-tripping. That's apparently how Rompe met our mojado: they were working double yellowheaded parrots plus an occasional scarlet macaw. This became a big bull market around the time that the Baretta television show peaked. Buyers competed to bid up parrot futures to unprecedented river highs.

Rompe and the wet would go down into the interior and dicker with the Indians who trapped parrots in the coastal jungles. "Make them young," they told their Indians. "For every young parrot you get a premium because those are easier to train. The maldito older ones are so wild, all they want to do is bite off an index finger." From the jungles of the interior the parrots traveled by fotingo to the Río Bravo. Rompe and the mojado would feed them a little bread soaked with pulque so that they would get drowsy and then they put them in a long flat cage that went atop a raft of inner tubes. Y pues, así no más. Facilito as Tzintzuntzan. They ran the river and picked up their van on the other side. From there to the parrot jobber who had orders on account from all over. There were birds for Houston oilers, Dallas bankers, Wichita ranchabouts, Norman, Oklahoma, academics and Chicago fashion plates.

In his prime our mojado was a grand sight. Dressed in a cordobés hat, finest Mexican leather hand-tooled boots, a Spanish bolero vest, with a superb pawn bolo tie fashioned from an old serpentine Tarahumara arrowhead studded with forty pieces of turquoise, he would find himself from time to time in Rosa's Cantina, lunching on short ribs soaked in red chile and catching up on the latest news from the Third World commodity market. When the city's Visitor and Convention Bureau decided to shoot a promo film he landed a bit part as the incarnation of Old Mexico. He looked like a Casasola sepia photograph of a 1910 Mexican revolutionary.

After sauntering to the post office or the telégrafos to wire some money to Sinaloa, he might, when business called for it, pack some clientes from out of town into his Winnebago and drive down to the zona de tolerancia where each bar had its own prostitutes licensed and medically supervised by the municipal authorities. Lots of college kids would be there mixed in with truckers, oil hands, ranchers, salesmen, other whatnot, and especially políticos. Our mojado didn't like to go there much. He didn't like the way the gabachos used the place as their pigpen. It seemed that a gabacho could be a faithful one-woman husband and church-going Elk or Moose in the coloso but once he crossed the border he figured he could paw, puke and otherwise make a fool out of himself with impunity. They were right. One night a well-heeled, distinguished looking black dude was trying to get laid. The hooker turned him down flat and suggested he try a lesser club down the street. It seemed that the management didn't cotton to the girls taking on black customers cause a class joint like theirs could start losing their gabacho clientele. El magnate was stunned. Jesus Christ, it was the last place in the world where he was expecting discrimination! He had to convince the puta that he was really a Puerto Rican grown up on the continent who had never learned Spanish. That made it o.k. and flushed with pride he paid his money and together they went on back.

Just one problemita. Anonymity was the virtuous precondition of transriver entrepreneurship in Mexérica. Or to paraphrase Heraclitus, a bandit oughtn't step into the same river twice. Our mojado began to earn himself a pretty big handle. While he had always stayed away from the aguas mayores, flesh and leaves in their various formats—these, under any account, being contolled by conglomerates of certain orders—even his long position in aguas menores was eventually compromised, and even undermined, by his air of haughty and driven defiance. A rural, Calderonian curandero of his propia honra, this mojado arrogated and amalgamated notions of robber bandit and Robin Hood even though he was riverwise enough to "know better." So then, while at the beginning his transgressions, when uncovered by the border patrol, were punished by the customary petty fines and slaps on the wrist—who really gets fired up about smuggling parrots or the prime ingredient in chewing gum?—his wet attitude of villano pero honrado quickly began to impress an indelible mark on the crowded, bored and hurried courtrooms where novelties could quickly be seized upon to alleviate the crushing monotonies imposed by the blur of contraband cohorts that filed past the judges' gavels. Similar was the attitude of the law enforcement community, some members of which apparently began to call him epithets like el superwet, el mojado en ajo, et alia. Our mojado noticed that his capture rate, which had an initial background level approximating a random walk, had risen off the charts to the point where at the close of his career it was more like an águila/sol tossup. He was worried, business was badly down, and his familia, now living in better quarters in Culiacán, began to voice remonstrations over larga distancia. But in misfortune too our mojado soberbio reveled in his own way, coming out of the bends in the river with parrots in his arms and an air of feverish anticipation (la migra ¿sí o no?), reliving in each crossing the river renaissance, this our San Juan Bautista, guardián de todos los mojados.

What is clearly apocryphal, claims el Rompeculos, yet certainly symptomatic in its being attributed to our bedeviled and vain-glorious mojado en ajo, was the so-called "wet warranty," which made its presence known for a few years around the time that Chrysler, G.M., and others promoted it in a different economic sector. The way it worked was that for a certain insurance premium the exporter of a commodity could in effect guarantee delivery of goods (or their dollar value) across the border irrespective of confiscations, water damage, dust storms, or acts of God. Indeed it was the "wet warranty" that destroyed el mojado's brokerage, which, given his high capture rate, could not afford to reimburse suppliers at any reasonable premium. Ni pedo, some insensitive souls blamed the new market circumstances on the arrogant mojado who indeed, while not a conceiver of the warranty, had, in a paradox that operates elsewhere in México (vid. Partido Revolucionario Institucional), attempted in a certain sense to institutionalize what had always been conceived as a peripatetic roll of the bones. Contrabandists began to mutter darkly (this, by the way, was during the period when Joe Columbo organized the Italian-American Civil Rights League and paid so dearly for his gesture) about the new affront to the truer days of caveat emptor, of river skullduggery, even as they had to comply with the economic writ of the period.

"Maldición. There are too many coyotes desgraciados who are making an effrontery of the perils of the river!"

"Precisamente. These pendejos are giving too high a profile to our dealerships."

Our mojado, like so many other Mexican revolutionaries and freethinkers over the decades, took a cue from caution. One moonless night, making sure he wasn't being tailed, he packed his personal belongings and drove to a place way upriver—a hardship spot with steep banks and a dearth of landing places, but one that also claimed the advantages of few sensors and virtually no patrol. He ran the river for one last time, never to return again.

Our mojado quickly descended from his comfortable bourgeois life into the vast anonimato of the undocumented worker. In a sense he wanted it and needed it that way. He shaved his Zapata mustache, cut his hair a different way, and took a humble job sorting remnants at a blue jeans manufacturer with an infamous reputation for its abuse of illegal aliens. He felt safe there;

he blended in. He cut off relations with everyone, even his family. It would only be a few months, he felt. His only connection was with his compadre, el Rompeculos.

Clearly la vida was softening up our pícaro for a spectacular conversion. Those forces of fate that redress Tex-Mex hubris were conspiring against our San Juan Bautista on two juxtaposed fronts. One was that the border entered into one of those sporadic periods when potentates in Washington become "deeply concerned." El mundo tightened up. There were delays on the International Amistad bridge for three and four hours. The United States Army Corps of Engineers busily installed a "tortilla curtain" to keep out illegal aliens, a reinforced steel mesh wall supposedly incapable of being cut but which was riddled with holes by sunup. The Border Patrol issued a list of persons it wanted to nab for high questioning, or rather, to pin some delitos to; payment was offered leading to the apprehension thereof, and our mojado made the list. His person became of some value and soon a co-worker in the remnant division of the factoría developed a certain inkling. The other factor, according to Rompe, must have been the "Huevos Whateveros."

"Huevos Whateveros," I asked him. "What the hell are those?"

"Third World food," said Rompe. "They're delicious. Let me share my own recipe. Take the remains of the last few nights of Mexican meals—chilaquiles, pico de gallo, frijoles refritos, ruptured enchiladas, a foresaken chile relleno and so on—and lard them into a deep frying pan. Add sufficient stewed tomatoes to obtain a brew and on top of this bubbling riverbed crack open as many eggs as called for, yolks intact. Over a low heat grate some braided Chihuahua cheese and sprinkle with as much cilantro, green onion, and epazote as coraje would prescribe. ¡Qué rico!"

"My God!"

"Well it probably was the huevos whateveros that gave him the tapeworms. After all, you can't use ingredients that are too stale or you run certain risks. At any rate, one day I received an emergency call from the mojado. Come at once! Can you believe it, the bridge was so tight with migra, aduana, fiscales, and the rest of that riffraff with their sniff hounds going through the gabachos' dirty underwear that I had to borrow my neighbor's water wings from his pool and cross the river that way. When I got to the mojado's I was confronted with a grotesque scene. A bull-necked, redneck Texan with a name like Bubba was directing his skeptical, Spanish-surnamed migra underlings who were gingerly stepping over the wet's vomit as they pulled on each of his arms. El mojado was pleading to be taken to the hospital. He was in the throes of calambres and slumgullion upchuck. The mojado's pet parrot (and if truth be known, only true companion over the years) was hysterical, ranging at full blast from the famous aria from *Figaro* to *La Cucaracha* to multiple pocho groserías.

"Hi there occifer! Where are you taking my compadre?"

"Haul off, scudsball! I'm taking this border bandito off to the slammer! He's on everybody's hit list, the Border Patrol, the Texas Rangers, the T-men, Batman and Robin, you name it. He must be a mastermind behind some Bolivian cocaine ring. Do you know how many times this shitheel has been up the river? Thirty-six count'em convictions, thirty-six!"

"Aw, come now occifer, don't hyberbolize. You know he's small potatoes. Why get so excited over a few lousy parrots that bring so much delight to lonely suburban housewives or a bargain basement lobster dinner for eight? Besides, I'm not asking you to let him go or nothin'. Put a ball 'n' chain on him for chrissakes but get him over to the hospital. If he's D.O.A. at patrol headquarters our trade association is going to hold you strictly to account." Rompe looked severely at the two Hispanos. "I see you two Judas-lackeys have gotten wetback barf on your Gucci loafers."

The scene at the hospital was no less poignant. The migra overlord stood fidgeting in the wings and growling into his walkie-talkie. The internist was chattering excitedly with the hospital administrator while Rompe sat with the mojado who, one hand on his underbelly, was in a state of stoic dejection.

"¿Por qué están tan excitados?" the mojado asked.

"No sé. El médico anda discutiendo con el jefe del hospital. No sé de que se trataría. Quizá de la migra."

"No, eso no es. Ha de ser que voy a morir al momento." The mojado was quickly becoming convinced that he was an accelerated terminal. A fitting dénouement for the life that he had lived.

The internist came over to the Mexicans. "Mr., uh . . . Mojado. It's not serious at all what you have. All they are are tapeworms.

Taenia saginata to be exact. They're fairly common in some parts of the underdeveloped world, but not at all common around here. Actually, they're pretty valuable. . . ." The internist looked disarmingly at the wetback. "I mean, not really valuable, but useful, experimentally useful."

The mojado looked at the doctor with incomprehension.

The internist turned to his compadre. "Go on, Mr., what's your name, Mr. Rompeculos."

"Diz que tienes gusanos. Diz que no te hacen daño y a lo mejor valen más que todo el oro de la mina de El Dorado."

The mojado brightened up measurably. He thought the worms in his body must be along the lines of Ponce de León's fabled elixir if they were worth their weight in golden nuggets.

The internist smiled ingratiatingly at the mojado. He made a little wriggling motion with his index finger as if it were a cutsie worm. "Sí, Mr. Mojado. That's right, el gusano."

The mojado smiled back and reciprocated with the same wriggling finger. "Oh, yes, meester doctor . . . the worm."

The internist turned to Rompe and explained the conditions of the barter. It seems that the hospital could put fresh specimens of taenia saginata to excellent use for their medical students. Fresh, living specimens—these would be so much better than mere mounted fantoches. Their medical students could be so much better prepared in the field of contagious diseases. Mr. Mojado would be doing a genuine service to society, a true charitable donation to the public weal. And incidentally, the doctor and the hospital administrator noticed that Mr. Mojado was having a bit of a problem with the Immigration Service? They were prepared to vouchsafe for Mr. Mojado, offer him a job on the spot as a matter of fact, nothing too strenuous of course, they couldn't . . . put any strain on their valuable flesh and blood test tube. All Mr. Mojado had to do was agree in writing to let them have . . . access to his tapeworms. They would do the rest.

By now the redneck had gotten very un-red. Images of a nice bonus and a commendation that had been dancing in his mind's eye were going under like a bloated, toxic catfish sinking into the Bravo for a third time. "Say here, doc, what do you mean about this felon being a worm factory or some kind of one-man maquiladora? This here border bandito's a known major criminal with 36 convictions and he's gotta be taken to justice. No way is he gonna be gainfully employed except maybe at the rock quarry!"

"Not true, not true!" shouted Rompe. "Worst he ever did was cross the river with a soused-up parrot. He's a fine citizen, sends all his income over to Culiacán where he's got a sick old father and twelve brothers and sisters."

"Well now, Mr. Bubba," said the hospital administrator. "I'm sure we can accommodate every one in this regard. We certainly think that your apprehension of this rascal should go recognized, and we'll help you see to that. But now that we've got him, let's give him some meaningful social role. Think, Mr. Bubba, this gentleman here, Mr. Mojado, can perform a vital function in the service of the public weal. As a matter of fact, and I'm sure you're not aware of this, your own chief of the Immigration Service is a patient of our head internist here, Dr. Buggy, whose helping him along with the duodenal ulcer that this frustrating wetback situation has brought on to him. Don't you see, it's with the experimental data that fellows like Mr. Mojado can provide that we may gain a real breakthrough and help you patrolmen out with medical solutions!"

The mojado had suffered another stomach spasm. Having no food left in him he had expectorated a small portion of phlegm mixed with blood. The hospital administrator snapped a finger and a silent indocumentado came out with a pail and mop (all the orderlies were wets, they were the only ones who could "afford" the pay). The doubled up mojado moved to face the internist. He pointed to his underbelly. "Is pain!"

"Oh, we'll take care of that, Mr. Mojado. Soon as you sign up with us we're going to give you a superb medicine that will control your tapeworms so that the pain will be just about eliminated. We need to control your supply of tapeworms, don't we sir? That's the essence of experimentation, isn't it, observation and control!"

"¿Qué dice?"

"Dice que si firmas te quedas aquí con una medicinita y si no te dejan morir de gusanitos hideputas o te llevan a la pinta o las ambas cosas a la vez."

"Dile que firmaré. Pero que me ayude. ¡Que me ayude!"

"He says he'll sign. But help, auxilio, socorro, amparo!"

"Mr. Mojado, I'm so glad that you are cooperating. I knew you would. I could tell you wanted to be of service to the community. Now, whenever you defecate, Mr. Mojado, you know, move your bowels (the internist made an indicative gesture with his hips), do so in a special vessel we'll be giving you. You see, the tapeworms are nested in your fecal matter."

"¿Qué dice?"

"Que tienes que cagar en una olla."

"¿En una olla?"

"Sí, es muy importante."

"Está bien. Lo hago. Con estos dolores cagaría en los cojones del Buda si fuese necesario." The spasm was easing and the mojado felt a little better. He had heard the word "fecal." It sounded like a place in the Yucatán where some time ago he had bartered for parrots. "¿Qué es, 'fecal'? El médico dijo, fecal."

"Es la caca."

"¿La caca?"

"Es la caca, es la mierda. Quieren que tú cagues en una olla para pizcar los gusanos que van a estar horadando en tu materia excremental."

The mojado was stunned. "¡Ay, fuchi!" He turned to the internist and pointed to his butt. "¿Fecal?"

"Sí, señor," the doctor replied and shyly patted the wet's ass. "Very valuable!"

"¡Mierda!"

"What's that, Mr. Mojado? No comprendo."

"¡Caca!"

The doctor looked quizzically at the mojado, then at Rompe and back at the mojado.

The mojado screamed at the top of his voice, "Eshit!"

The internist blushed. "My, señor Mojado! You do speak pretty good English after all. I think your English is much better than my Spanish!

Burn out. The last six hours on the bus together we spent in a restless hush. A half hour in front of Ajo, Arizona, the sun had risen over the desert. There is no finer color to the desert, no finer air than that of a desert dawn. We were by the Organ Pipe

Cactus National Monument and here and there the sun shone through the giant flowering saguaro cacti and through the iron-wood trees that seemed like dwarfs in comparison.

"You'll be off this bus in minutes, Rompe, and into a cup of fresh coffee. That'll be nice."

"Yeah, Huitla. Appreciate passing spirits and gas with you. There is one last thing I ought to tell you though."

"What? That you are the mojao?"

He looked startled. "How'd you know that?"

"I guess it was your impassioned grasp of details. Also, a no-name mojao. Más sabe por viejo que por diablo, right?"

"God damn!" He punched my arm affectionately. "That's right, you clever college vato."

"You still into tapeworms?"

"Hell no! Those nasty little critters! I got out of that indentured servitude some years ago. Learned English real good—I'm even a resident of the coloso now. I mean, I'd never become a U.S. citizen, but I'm strictly legit. I've seen the re-Hispanization of the deep Southwest over these two decades or so, the demographic effects of migration, the palpable result of raza versus Anglo birth rates, the Hispanic changeover of officials ranging from mayors to county clerks and police officers. I used to think that it all meant the reconquest of the Southwest by the Republic of México, gradually and in evolutionary increments. Now I realize it's another thing, a new patrimony that is more than the mere sum of its parts, the Third World." He laughed. "Maybe we ought to join with you college intelligentsia vatos and call it Aztlán.

"That would be fine with me, Rompe."

"Yeah, but it would be quite an undertaking, wouldn't it? Students and river runners, hand in hand? We'll do it quiet, in desert stealth, right? No use building up big recognition. A rep could be bad for this border. Although, I don't think anything except maybe a totally East German goose-stepping mentality could put a real lid on the Bravo."

"What about the family back home?"

"Good, ése. Consuelo's 32 now and she's still not married or anything. Isn't that grand? She's thinking of taking her dowry and entering el convento. Never in our maddest dreams did anyone in our family figure that one of us could have the lana to enter the Church. Or maybe she'll marry after all, maybe to some gente de bien, alguien de villarica. It's her choice."

The bus was pulling into the parking lot of the Ajo Cantina and Grille. Rompe whispered in my ear, "You know what I'm really here for? I'm into running cactus. It's strictly part time, but it's real good bread, a seller's market. I've got a bandit run going for two 60 foot saguaros. Got a big rig loaded and waiting. I understand some outfit like Bank of America or American Express wants them for the front office grounds. Hay que cumplir, ¿verdad? Hell, cactus—pound for pound there's more money in them than coca leaves. And nobody, and I mean nobody's gonna bother you about a cactus. What's the worst it's gonna do you? A few stray thorns in your paw?"

"Wear heavy gloves, ése."

"Now you're talking, vato habilidoso. ¡Cógelo suave! Ai te huacho."

He walked out of the Trailways bus with his cocky air of rustic indio vergüenza and coraje.

I thought as I sat back in my seat, immediately missing his camaraderie, that they had taken much from the Rompemojado. They had taken his loved ones, his puberty, his sense of honor and of shame, his indio way of life, his mother tongue, and the very fruit of his bowels. But they had given him uniquely new family ties, a sense of coraje and varonía, a novel-fashioned lengua, a Third World identity and a river baptism in fire. Add up each column, then, and call it a waterworks wash.

And then, finally, there was the matter of the fecal matter— the aguas mayores. It's not every hombre who can claim his turd as a deduction to the common weal.

The Raza Who Scored
Big in Anáhuac

I thought, being raza, that this was my tierra. You know, roots, ¡qué sé yo! Now I think maybe I'm just another extranjero, one who crossed the wrong-way river.

I came down to learn stuff. Junior term in Anáhuac. At the Universidad Nacional Autónoma—the student movement—¡la revolución estudiantil!—I met and befriended Felipe Espinoso. He helped me with my notes because, speaking frankly, my written castellano isn't the best. "Language loss" is what some professor once muttered to me when I tested out at Cal State. Felipe was curious about Chicano ways. He called me "güero valín, the Mexican in preppie polo shirts." That made me laugh and I would kid him about the same Yucatecan guayabera that he wore every day that I knew him. We were both attending the same course, Theory and Practice of Mexican Social Class Structure, taught by tal profesor, one Maximiliano Peón, who alerted us at once to the fact that even though his remuneration was not enough to cover the gasoline that the trip cost him, he was proud to be teaching this course at UNAM as a servicio to the youth of his patria.

From the profile Felipe reminded me—it was an uncanny, almost perfect likeness—of a Mayan head in Palenque, a bas-relief with the prominent Mayan nose and receding forehead that I had pondered over in an art book at the Cal library. I had always wanted urgently to visit Palenque. I used to think about its gothic arches and cornstalk glyphs when I was just a kid, working behind the counter at the Taco Bell, baking cinnamon crispas. Now I found myself in Anáhuac, peering into the eyes of a Maya.

Felipe pressed me hard on Aztlán, and pleased with his avid interest, I was proud to tell him about the meaning of César

Chávez' black águila in a white circle, of vato and cholo, the Sleepy Lagoon riots, the finer points of pachuquismo, the fate of Reies Tijerina, the difference between an acto and a mito, Los Angeles street murals, and the old Operation Wetback of the '50s and the silly Tortilla Curtain que parió.

In turn, I queried him about the political peripecias of Vicente Lombardo Toledano, the pastimes of Siquieros when they threw him in the Lecumberri lockup, the subtleties redounding in the national diversion of deciphering every six years who the PRI tapado really was, the new malinchista movement of contemporary Mexican feministas, what Buñuel had really meant in *Los olvidados*, and why Cantinflas had plastic surgery done on his notable nose.

One afternoon after class, at the tortería which surely has the best crema in the valley of Mexico, La Tortería Isabela la Católica, only a few minutes from the University library which is a living historico-revolutionary mural, I confided in him a Chicano hope for a binational carnalismo. We were both brought to tears and to a heartfelt abrazo de correligionarios, not to mention compinches.

In class Felipe Espinoso was quiescent. Weren't we all? In our aula there were over 80 where there should have been 50. The earliest got seats, the next earliest, window sills, then came those who pressed along the walls until the door could no longer be opened and the half dozen hapless laggards who either missed the lecture of the day or tried to catch a semblance of the proceedings from outside, through a window. The University had been built for 120,000 almas; there were over 260,000 in attendance. Classes had been scheduled seven days a week from the earliest morning until midnight.

During the days approaching registration, Indians trod in from the valley, from the mountains surrounding the valley, from the plains beyond the mountains which circle this Anáhuac. They filed down the mountain roads, dog-tired, without chavos or any other material resources, spurred on by an implacable will for wisdom and upward mobility. Alentados perhaps by rural maestras de escuela they came for the term to UNAM where tuition was basically free. They traveled the roads in huaraches made from the rubber of discarded tires, slept where they could, in attics, hidden in obscure recintos of the university, in the swimming pool when there was no water, waited resignedly for a seat to study in the hopeless library that could no longer accommodate the push of the masses, begged or hustled for the term's nourishment. I have seen this drive that cannot be stemmed by any earthly privation or police state curtain at my heartfelt border, across which God's innocent children slip into the promised coloso of milk and miel, and I genuflect before these campesino multitudes and each day relive their fierce, steadfast resolve, share their dusty anger, revere their pursuit of self-improvement.

Halfway into the course, Felipe made a pronouncement. "Güero, I thought I liked Prof. Maximiliano Peón. I no longer like him. He is a deception. He is pequeño burgués."

"He comes out here for nothing to teach this unwashed horde and untouched rabble, doesn't he?"

"Sure, he comes out, and punctually. He's all subjectivity and nineteenth-century retórica, spouting about the incontrovertible objective realities of Marxist-Leninist revolutionary materialism. He's a living contradiction, a comfortable gentilhombre, an hidalgo of the professorate, all immersed in bourgeois pieties and comforts, drunk with arriviste parfums and amaretto and frangelico liquors. But to assuage his sotted, corrupted soul, to aggrandize his smug persona, to allay his midnight anxieties— because he knows well that his kind and his class would be first to the paredón in a genuine revolution—he sacrifices salary and comes out here to provoke Inditos de Lerdo Chiquito so that they may march to revolutionary beats, so that they may be mowed down by imported burp guns. Yes, he'll watch it all on his Magnavox in the parlor. He'll be hoping that he's hedged every bet, that he'll come out triumphant no matter who wins the partido."

I should confess now that Felipe was a fanatic for the Jai Alai and he had taught me to be a fanatic. His frontón imagery troubled me. Of course it was what everybody tried to do at the Jai Alai, bet on the underdog when the price was low and hope for the score to turn, then bet again on the opposing team at good odds and sit out the game a sure winner no matter which team won. . . . I protested, "But I love his Spanish! My God, his command of language!"

"¡Coño! Sure you do. You're a poor, hapless Chicano—a güero pocho boy who has never had the opportunity to study your mother tongue with any formality or system until now. Don't

be deceived. It's all Porfirian sophistry and pedagogical petti-
foggery. He doesn't even speak Spanish anyway. He speaks
Castilian. And these poor, ingenuous indios—I include myself
here, once a poor simpleton from Quintana Roo—who also are
mostly tonguesmen of Zapoteca, Huichol, or whatever, they are
mesmerized by this castizo buffoon who wishes to provoke their
action for lost causes so he can feel assuaged for having 'done
something about the Mexican social class problem.'

"This is wrong," he went on. "Let us have a revolution in Ol-
meca, or Chichimeca, or Náhuatl even, or Mayaquiché. Anything
but the Porfirian castellano of the Mexican empire and the simper-
ing sleight of hand of the crypto-revolutionary."

So, then, Maximiliano fell from his pedestal. But who or what
to replace him with?

The Virgin of Guadalupe's day was approaching. We were
tertuliando with other left-leaning student intellects at a café
in the slanting sun on the Promenade of Institutionalized Revolution, near the cathedral. We could see a pilgrimage approaching like marabunta down the wide promenade. Felipe told me
that tonight would be a fine one to be at the Jai Alai. Probably
he should take all my money and his too and bet it on the main
partido.

"Why is that, Felipe?"

He turned to the Promenade. "They will be betting heavy."
The pilgrimage swept down the Promenade, eighteen campesinos
abreast, marching in for the novena. There were delegations from
Tenancingo and Tlaxcala, Acámbaro and Acatlán, Pátzcuaro
and Pachuca, and even Pénjamo and Tzintzuntzan. First the
crests of cyclists congruous to paramilitants. They had plastic
virgins tacked to their handlebars and wheels and pennants that
saluted the breeze of their own making. Then came legions of
dusty benditos, huffing and chanting the Ave María, each village
headed by a priest and an icon. Then down the Promenade of
Institutionalized Revolution came herds of goats and turkeys and
aggressive geese, bullied by trotting boys and mongrels. The
peddlers followed too, hawking tostadas in green or red sauce,
sweet potatoes in carts with piercing steam whistles, guava and
cajeta, mamey and mango ice, jícama in vinaigrette. Jesting and
cursing in the militant sun the pilgrims marched and peeled corn
husks, smearing the tender grain of their elotes with colored

sauce. On the special earthen track, the last kilometer to the cathedral doors, the supplicants came by on bloody knees, bearing the indrawn vision. In the courtyard they were doing Amerindian dances against the slanting, sinking cathedral walls. Precisely every ten meters hung white metal signs with red letters neatly stenciled: It is strictly forbidden to urinate against these holy walls.

That night at the Jai Alai with all our funds in hand I worried and became a little drunk. Felipe doubted too and wondered if we oughtn't be at the cockfights. "On nights of the novena the Indians come to the cock arena and wager nuggets of gold that they have dug out of the countryside."

"But here too the galleries are filled with countryfolk. Besides, Felipe, we are fanatics for the Jai Alai. We know nothing of cockfights."

"True enough. All I know of the cocks is that they use one straight and one curved dagger. That's all I know. It's a question of breeders and other intimate variables." Felipe sighed. "Whatever happens tonight, we cast our lot with the people."

"Sure," I said. Right then I felt muy raza, muy Mexican. "Sí, con el pueblo." But immediately I started to wonder. "Do you think the games are fixed?"

"Who would fix them for the poor to win?"

"Maybe the government. On orders of the authority."

"I wouldn't put that beyond the authorities. A devious scheme to enervate the pilgrims. But no. Why should the government subsidize the gambling vice? Besides, it doesn't happen all the time. It's just . . . a pattern. We must realize that by probability we stand to lose. But the odds make it worthwhile. A handsome wager."

"But I don't want to lose, Felipe. If I lose I will have to eat pinto beans all month. I'll have to return to Califas."

Felipe laughed. "Come now, compis. It's not every day that a vato loco can wager with the people with a firm hand. Maybe the match is fixed every night before the pilgrims make the final march to celebrate Tepeyac. Just to brighten the Indian's firm belief in the miraculous. But no, I don't think there's any question of a fixed game. It's simply the milieu, those days when the campo and the aldea come to court, the Indians packed in the galleries, hiding behind masks. I think it's a spirit that descends on the Jai Alai court. An ether which comes from the galleries and penetrates the players."

"Perhaps a revolutionary spirit?"

"Yes, but lapped up by the gambling vice the way mole is contained and dammed by corn dough. The inditos make their way up to the galleries expecting the supernatural."

I laughed. "What would Gramsci think of this, Pablo Freire, even the barbudo Carlos Marx? Could they construct a paradigm pa'l fenómeno?"

"Hard to say. It's too early in the course."

"You're right, Felipe. On a night like tonight one should be a Jai Alai fanatic. Have you seen all the grenaderos about?"

"Yes. They've even brought a contingent in from Atzcapotzalco. I'm sure there are two in front of every pulquería, every brothel, every revolutionary square, every Ateneo in Mexico City."

"How many do you think there are at the University library, underneath the mural?"

Saturday night at the Palacio de la Pelota, El Frontón México. The Jai Alai court was stretched and wide, bounded by three rock walls. The open end was strung with an immense steel net protecting the spectators from the missiles. Occupying the choice seats in the middle of the stands were the vested ones, Arabs and Jews, gachupines and wealthy Mexicans who played the favorite and lapped up the chiquitero money.

There was a roar from the crowd. The intendant and four huge Basques with long straw wickers bound to their wrists entered the court. They marched single file and solemnly along the wood boundary line. Then they turned and faced the crowd, placed their wickers across their hearts in salute, and gave the slightest of nods. There were whistles, jeers, and enthusiastic applause. The players broke rank and began to practice up. It was two mean frisky bucks playing against two stooping esthetes.

Felipe studied the program. "This match is a timeless syndrome: youth versus experience. Only a poet or saint will win this."

"Well then," I asked. "Who do we bet on?"

"It doesn't matter, güero. The team that falls behind and permits the chiquiteros to bet their pittances. We will bet on the underdog, the people, and their expectations for a miracle."

"I like that, Felipe. A higher logic. I may be a vato loco but you are a vate loco. A meta-wager and a melodrama. A dialectic that ends in a materialistic. I like the pastel money of México. It's easier than the hardened green of the dólar."

Redcaps called the odds out, which were an even 100 red versus 100 blue, and the match to 30 points began. The fierce bucks dominated from the very start and as the score mounted in their favor the odds dwindled, 50, 30, 10 to 100. From the galleries there was a steady projection of sullen mirth.

I saw an Olmec-looking type call out, "That old camel should be playing marbles with his grandchild!" and a striking mestizo who looked the prototype of Vasconcelos' raza cósmica imprecated a few times and then said, "Get him a pair of roller skates . . . and a seeing-eye dog!" Rejoined a weasel who looked more like the critics of Vasconcelos who coined a raza cómica, "No, old fool! Bring him Sancho Panza!"

The score was 20 to 12. The redcaps had become bored and sat in the aisles kibitzing with their clients. The guards, instead of standing straight up, were lounging on the very net that bounded the court. And the sharks filed their teeth or counted their fistfuls of wagers on short odds or nonchalantly cracked sunflower seeds. That was when we bet most of the money credited to us for a month of studies and livelihood on the underdog at 80 to 1000. The sharks were glad to take our money. "No lo hagan," a concerned bourgeois gentilhomme advised us. "You're just going to make a tiburón happy. ¡Que el partido se va de calle!"

A portentous occurrence. The Jai Alai became like the opera buffa. The old artistes made two points and there was an ominous silence. The redcaps got up from the aisles but called out few odds. There was almost no betting. They were waiting—the galleries and the short money, seven, eight thousand strong—for another mysterium. The intereses creados squirmed up in their chairs like weasels. This point—it was taking too long, too many volleys! The great and turning point came in like high tide and the redcaps quieted nor scuffles nor coughs but the pok of the rubber and rocklike sphere impacted and spread upon the front wall and the long, retrograde arc of the orb obfuscating in spotlights, the skim of wrists along the green middling and the crack of stone's conjunction with straw. Rolando, the stiff yet still graceful elder, scooped up the ball on the short hop and propelled it swan's neck thick on the middle so it angled sinuously on the low wide front, bounced within the far outside wood and spiraled into the netting. The galleries were ripped wide open with Amerindian joie de vivre. The men or beasts within tore asunder their poses and stepped outside themselves. The promised sign! I turned to Felipe. He glowed with cherubic ecstasy. I held his head like a son. The redcaps called out odds: 40 to 100, make it 45, no, 50 to 100. Red and blue tickets passed countless brown hands. The aisles writhed like serpents. We bore the manic coaster to allegorical heaven.

It was like the Westerns too. The well-off villains in their business suits and gold pocket watches presenced their reserved finale. They put away their pepitas and pistachios and their eyes popped and jaws hung awry. "Cover!" they begged the redcaps. They wanted to cover, to hedge. The God-fearing rested easy. None of us doubted the outcome. Social and poetic justice would be done.

Rolando was all about, luxuriating in his renaissance, his regained nerve.

Soon we were winning! The young bucks leaned against the wall and slowly sank to the floor, their innards chafing, their tongues flapping. Holding his wicker high above him like a torch, Rolando traversed the court with the stately mockery of a ceremonious bullfighter. Caught up in the euphoria I began to scream a confused litany of mythic templates. The eagle, the serpent, the nopal, the thunderbird, the ¡Sí se puede!, la MECHA, el Anáhuac, Aztlán, all jumbled in the same olla. Felipe and I embraced. "¡Vamos a ganar! ¡Venceremos!"

Then, an inexplicable alteration of events. The elders loosened up—¡que se aflojaron!—got tired, and permitted the youngsters to come back. The game tied up at 29. The ultimate metaphysic! Peepee was drawn from the caved-in bladders of many. The galleries lost their nerve and hastened to hedge their spleens. The sharks and businessmen, anxious to reduce their losses, covered the Indians and bet all the Rolando they could. The redcaps shrieked out the odds, 100 even, 100 pesos, pick'em.

I grabbed Felipe. "Los indios have lost their nerve and are seeking insurance. ¡Tienen los huevos en la garganta!"

"Me too!"

"Let's cover! If we do, we win either way!"

"No way," Felipe said, "let us ride!"

I was in a swoon. "Oh, God! All that pastel!"

"Are you with me?"

I squeezed his hand. My knees were buckling. His face was mauve and bloated. "God, yes!"

I am an innocent, I thought. The ingenuous fanatic. For the moment I loved him so I could have given him my life.

The ultimate point began.

Rolando served the ball, a giveaway straight to the opposing frontman. We should have lost, instead the ball dribbled obscenely out of the unnerved wicker.

"We won!"

The young buck climbed and clawed the net in a twist of fury. Futile as Bergman's squire.

I turned to Felipe. "You won! You knew the old boy'd do it!"

He didn't seem terribly happy, though. He pointed at Rolando leaving for the dressing room, wiping his brow amid hosannas. "It took a lot out of him."

I felt funny. Felipe and I split the money, 50-50. The devalued pastel wad of Mexican money barely entered my pocket. I had more in the wallet. There were bills in my shirt pocket. Child supplicants stood willfully at the exit to the Palacio. I emptied coins into each calloused hand.

"Don't do that," he said.

"Why not?"

"It's bad form. It makes you look like a gringo."

"I know that. It's only because tonight I've scored big."

"No, never. You'll spoil them."

To win money: that was not enough. Felipe was still angry, knotted up by the match, and slowly I became angry too. It was not enough on the eve of the Virgin's day, despite the magnificent catharsis. Why? No más por no más.

Felipe had been silent while we lined up and collected our bets. Now he almost whined. "Now we must go and fuck some woman. I know a brothel, not too far."

"I don't want to fuck some woman! I'm too buoyant. I want to keep my money. Not tonight, Felipe. I'm too worn."

"Pues sí, compis. That's the way we do things here. The night won't be complete. El rito del Jai Alai se lo exige."

"I thought you were a poet, a mystic, and a left-leaning intellectual."

Felipe cursed a lot about shitting in the milk of the Virgin and all that folklore. "If you win, you've got to go. Don't leave me to my designs."

"What's this brothel like?"

"Perverse! What güero can claim to have known México without having visited its muchachas?"

"What do you mean, perverse?" I asked him hostilely.

He grinned. "Authentically perverse."

La Madama Lulú's was not perverse. It was repulsive, y me pareció muy típico. Two grenaderos sat on the sidewalk in front of the brothel. Some político or máximo chingón was fucking his brains out. Their carbines lay on the pavement at their sides. They winked at us as we went in. The brothel bureaucrats sat us on an overstuffed Louis XVI and the whores lined up and flaunted us all petite soirée fête in stained miniskirts. "¡Vamos a hacer beibis!"

I didn't have the huevos to choose so the most entrepreneurial of their lot plopped on my thighs and fondled my member. Soon, having been kneaded like a croissant, it began to acquire that mauve, belligerent feel. "Ven aquí," she coaxed. She took some of my salmon and sandía-colored money and gave it to the bookkeeper. The bookkeeper gave me a red poker chip. Then I had to give the poker chip to the porter who meticulously opened the door to a broomcloset cubicle and handed me a roll of toilet paper. We went inside. I didn't give a shit anymore. ¡Qué carajos! I was resolved. Yet suddenly I realized I was fucking a perfect stranger.

Later we were famished. The high was worn and it had turned cold and raw. There were pilgrims wandering the street, like strays. Felipe and I went to an all-night estancia where they cut newspapers into napkins. We had steaming hot caldo tlalpeño. We had machitos, finely minced tacos of bull testicles sprinkled with aguacate and cilantro in piquant sauce, sympathetic cannibalism. We washed it down with Carta Blanca. Felipe was quiet and grave. He looked frightened. I couldn't fathom what he was thinking.

I kept drinking. After a while I asked him, "Why don't men

and women do anything or go anywhere together in this country? Why are the men in the plaza and the women en casa?"

"They do go out together," he protested.

"Sure, to a té danzante at five in the afternoon."

"Those are appropriate hours. I'm sorry that we are not as advanced as your civilization."

"I've told you before, Felipe. It's not my civilization. Shit, I just live there. Don't blame me you sent out a fuck-up like Santa Anna to do an hombre's job."

"Here we still believe in the novia santa."

"You do?"

"Sure."

"I mean you, Felipe Espinoso from Quintana Roo."

"Why not?"

"It seems muy raro. I bet. The novia santa. It goes well with la casa chica."

"Don't insult me."

"I'm sorry. You have a novia waiting for you?"

"Sure."

"Where?"

"In Tulúm. It's small."

"Sure, I know it. There are ruins there. Hay presencia del pasado."

"Tienes razón."

"And how long since you've seen her?"

"The six years I've been here at the University. I take a course and a course and a course. Como tu work-study, right?"

"Not quite. You're going to marry her?"

"As soon as I graduate."

The night was cool and Mexican. Stars appeared like wishes. It was very still, soon it would be early. We walked with our hands in our pockets and our faces down, steadfast in the drunken ambience. We came to a park. The coconuts and the palms were still and etched. Some campesinos with no place to go were trying to sleep on the benches that they had arrogated. There was suddenly a clump of grass in front of me. I plopped on it. The grass tickled my nostrils. I giggled.

"Get up!" Felipe sounded alarmed. He pulled me. It seemed like someone else's arm.

"¡Viva la revolución!"

"Be quiet, won't you!"

"What do you mean, quiet? Is this a police state? ¡Viva la revolución! ¡Viva la virgen de Tepeyac! ¡Viva Tonantzín! Let every good fellow now join in this song, Vive la companie. Good health to each other and pass it along, Vive la companie."

"Get up!"

"No, you come down. Down to my level."

"All right. If you quiet down."

I laughed. "Where I live they say Mexicans—that means Chicanos of course, not you real Mexicans—were made to pizcar tomates because they're built low to the ground. What do you think about that?"

He flashed his winning grin. "I'm curious about your Chicano ways."

"Well. When are you going to graduate?"

"Soon, if you keep quiet so no one steals my money tonight."

"Did you walk to Mexico City from Tulúm?"

"Well, no. Actually, I got an aventón."

"And were you like the indios that come streaming in from the picos and the valles around registration time?"

"Most assuredly."

"And did you live like them, begging, and hustling, and working?"

He smiled. "Well, nobody gets to find much work in this city."

"So then?"

"So I'm still hustling. Only I'm an advanced student now, senior class."

"¿Qué me dices?"

"I'm sorry, güero. We were playing only with your pastel money."

"Only my money? But I saw you pitch in your share."

"That was merely sleight of hand."

"I see. So then, at 29 up, you weren't really that nervous."

"Oh, I was very nervous."

"Yeah, but not as nervous as me."

"No, I wouldn't think so."

"No, you wouldn't think so. After all, for you it was win or tie."

"Something like that."

"And you don't feel bad?"

"I feel very bad. I need for you to know how bad I feel, even now, after winning, despite winning. Not only the money, but my life's dream, enough to live on so that I can take a full course of study and graduate. Porque, compis, tú eres mi cuate, ¿sabes? O, como dicen los tuyos, soy tu carnal."

"How can you say this shit to me now? Do you know I'm debating whether or not to kick your fucking head in?"

"Pues, ponte chango, carnal. Pa' la próxima más aguzao, vato. Porque ya aprendiste. That's what Buñel meant in *Los olvidados*. Like they say in these parts, más cornadas da el hambre que el toro."

"Don't hand me that pestilent shit. You simply hustled me. I'm just as poor as you. You knew if I lost that match I would probably have had to drop out and return home. Either that or starve."

"And you're not used to starving. Sure you're poor—I realize that. But you work. As a stock boy, at Taco Bell, as a piss pot polisher. Lo que sea, entran los chavitos, haga cola para el financial aid. You're poor like Cheech and Chong. We use the same word, poor, but we don't mean the same referent. I mean devastated, a nullity without the remotest identity."

"Why are you telling me all this stuff now? You won your ticket. Why couldn't you have just let me keep on thinking you were a fucking prince?"

"Pues, por pura vergüenza. You may not believe it: allí en la casa de putas, where much profound Mexican thought takes form, I thought about it long and hard. But you deserve more. You are a fine fellow, very young, ingenuo, and my sense of shame and your need to know, they joined forces. It may not be as pretty as pastel illusions or the half breed Virgin who showed herself to the cosmic race, but I felt I owed you the truth. Por eso bajaste al Anáhuac, ¿no?"

"And besides, you have enough money now, ¿verdad? You've got your graduation ticket and you can give up your contingency pigeon, right?"

He looked crestfallen. "I'm sorry. Los malos hábitos are difficult to overcome. I want to go to school intensively now and graduate and no longer do what I used to have to do."

"Well, I guess the course is over. It's been . . . well, it's definitely been a learning experience."

"Get up, güero, please."

"Why should I? I want to sleep. Here, entre las palmas."

"They won't let you sleep here. Some grenaderos will come by. They'll take you to the station and keep the pastel money which you think is so much softer than the dollar."

The grass began to smell of manure. I got up.

On the ninth day I discovered I had contracted the gonk. That was quite a letdown. The same day the pilgrims returned to the countryside and the grenaderos abandoned the University library with its revolutionary mural. I watched the campesinos as they trod out of the capital. The drunken revel was over and so was the holy fervor. They were tired, broke, bearing loathsome lesions on their knees that peered out of their trousers, which had worn away in their penitent sojourn to the Virgin's sanctuary. They looked like a crestfallen army in retreat. They resembled those Vietnamese multitudes on the run that we used to look at, guilt-ridden and repulsed, on the evening news.

When the last of the campesinos and their geese had moved on I could then cross the Promenade of Institutionalized Revolution to the barrio pharmacy where they were caring for me. All my money seemed to be dissipating in penicillin and in little luxuries to assuage the discomfort. Every day I walked sore and open-legged to the pharmacy and pulled down my trousers in the back room. The attendant, una celestina fea y arrugada who looked like the incarnation of gleeful disapproval, would put the needle in.

"How many cc's are you going to give me?"

"You need a million cc's this time up."

"No chingues. You'll have the needle in my bun for over five minutes. It'll be an hour before I'll be able to move my leg."

"¡Cómo que no chingues! That's what *you* should say to yourself, güerito. ¡Porque chingue y chingue y mira el resultado! O como decimos por aquí: Quien se acuesta con pulgas . . ."

"Spare me the dénouement. Let's get it over with. Look, why don't you just give me 500,000?"

"You want 500,000? I'll give it! You know how many machos come back here three weeks later, open-legged and bawling because the pus is back again and dripping out of their putrid chiles?"

"God no, give me the million. Anything."

"Here it goes, y no chilles, ¿eh? güerito valín. Porque como sabes, tú tienes la enfermedad de los meros machos." She began to laugh with great moral gusto. As my leg turned numb I realized that in Mexico the man wasn't always in the plaza and the woman only en casa.

It was just a few days before my term was up and I was to return to Califas. I bumped into Espinoso in the library.

"Hola, vate loco."

He looked embarrassed, almost searching for a space to slink into. "Hola, vato loco. It's been some days since I've seen you."

"Well, yes, I've been spending time at the old farmacia. I got the gonk, thanks to you and your macho ideas and your disgusting putas that you believe are sensuously perverse."

"Well, I figured. I got it too. La mierda de gonorrea is epidemic here."

"Well, that's the best fucking news I've heard all week!"

"You think so? You want to reenact the Alamo here in the library? Fuck it, man, be happy it's just gonk que se quita con penicilina and not what they say you get on the other side of the river, herpes. Let me tell you something, güero, and this is God's truth. Since I've been here, six years in this hostile valley, that was the first time I got laid."

"Not enough billetiza, right?"

"Right. It wasn't a financial priority."

"Sure, you didn't have a sufficiently dumb gringo to hustle big enough at the Jai Alai. Well, you must be busted by now what with shots and poultices and all. Here, let me stake you again— what the fuck, the Chicano baboso never learns." I flipped out a pink and canary bill with the likeness of Venustiano Carranza and stuffed it in his guayabera pocket.

"I'll accept it as a wedding present on behalf of my novia and me."

"Yeah. I was sure that you'd accept it o.k., Mr. Savoir Faire."

"I don't mean to hurt you, güero valín. But, ¿sabes lo que tú eres . . . en el fondo?"

"No, Mr. Maya. No idea what I am en el fondo. But I'm sure you're gonna tell me, Mr. Sabelotodo."

"En el fondo tú eres . . . ¡turista!"

Time softens the sense of injury and lets the little nostalgias form the veins and lodes that make the past palatable. If I had an address to write to, I would have sent him a card or something. But there was no address, maybe the empty swimming pool, o como dijo esa noche, una nulidad sin identidad remota, and barring that I would find myself in the State library, which seemed like an unsullied cavern, to sit and ponder, open the page in the art book to the Palenque man, frame ideas, sometimes talk silently to the stone head.

When you give meaningful events the profound reflection that they require, the many details that you missed in the ongoing come into relief and give a new bent to the hurt. In the labyrinthine library of my soledad I uncovered and relived the discreet portents and signs. How he envied and admired attributes that I didn't remotely realize. Güero, he called me, though in this country I could not remotely pass for fair. And my blue jeans and knitted polo shirt were such a center of attraction, the ballpoint pen that contained three cartridges, red, black, and green. Finally, I gave it to him. The way he liked to introduce me to girls on the campus—girls, I conclude now, who were not his friendly acquaintances as I had thought at the time, but barely accorded him the minimal courtesies of fellow studenthood. He would introduce me, I realize now, with a touch of the panderer, and how they would take to the exotic Chicano, the güero valín with a rather hairy chest who maybe reminded them in his knit shirt of some phantasm image they had conjured in their head, a Robert Redford, well-heeled, privileged and native in Spanish. You were waiting there, Felipe, furious and sotted with envy, bridling your lust— how you must have kept so much venom under wraps—hoping that I would puncture the maiden ethics of niñas bien, maybe score, maybe there would be a scrap of carrion in it for you. For you hadn't been laid in six years!

How you queried me, Maya, about so many things like routes and rivers, fences and sensors, coyotes and pollos. Were you trying on Chicano, my friend? Were you speculating on the North? How proud you were, como un tío paternal, when you arranged a little public trial for me at the tortería, bade me eat the chile más pequín de la tortería. And when I passed your little test and won a round of student applause did you not say, see, he's no gringo now, he's earned his bones. But it was nothing! I've been eating those pequines my whole life!

Now I feel so mortified that I could have confided in you—

¿qué?—after two or three days of acquaintanceship at most, such
intimate yearnings as my whole carnal hope for Mexican-Chicano
compañerismo. ¡Qué ingenuo! Now I know, máximo peón, that
even in oppression, even if there are only two oppressed peas in a
constricted pod, they will disaggregate into an oppressor and an
oppressed, a siervo and a señor, a leader and a led. That is the
nature of oppression and of the oppressed, the theory and the
practice. That they know only what they know and act on what
they know, a great chain of oppressed people, a great daisy chain
of being that leads not straight to St. Thomas' sandía-hued heav-
en, but low, up and down picos, down and up valleys, across
llanos and even across rivers where the current runs in opposing directions. Yet, truly escarmentado that I am for having so
readily and unselfconsciously confided in El Otro, that moment
in the tortería, that heartfelt abrazo over tortas de lomo . . . How
is it that two oprimidos of such divergent estirpes, of such varied
formation, could have, if just for a transitory term, communed? I
cherish that shared governance of perceptions even though to
obtain it requires a racking sojourn into memories filled with peni-
tence and humiliation. And I think of a passage in Hemingway
where it is observed that where we are weak, there nature surely
breaks us, and if we fare with good fortune, and go on the mend,
there where we were weak we are now the strongest. And although in the end it's all the same for nature will break us, defin-
itively, it will not be at the junction where once we were weak and
now we are strong.

Amigo, I don't quarrel with your many truths nor the intensity
of your motives. Of one thing, no cabe duda, I am poor like
Cheech and Chong—thank God for it, bless that level of poverty
that still subsidizes the notion of humorous solutions.

Well yes, there is one perception that I quarrel with. ¡Yo no
soy turista! In truth you were the tourist, amigo, as well as the tour
guide and the conning lout. A most engaging and eager one, the
way you genuinely investigated my nature, but like any tourist,
even an enlightened and avid one, you compared the landscape
by a self-same standard. Your sense of the picturesque, the empa-
thetic, and the offensive were all measured out in the same pastel
currency. But the estranged is different from the tourist. It is his
lot to wander forth, to cross rivers that flow up course, seek out
his own image in the dubious landscape of the other, search for

a currency that isn't there. Por supuesto, the Chicano needs to gaze into smoky mirrors that reflect no peer. Know this, venerable Maya head that has perdured for 1200 years on a coated ivory page in a slick art book in a State library: I am strong where I've been broken and I'm not prepared to cave in.

Mocha in Disneyland

When you are swinging in the Swiss Family Treehouse in the midst of a starry Anaheim night, listening to the random baying of Disneyland's hounds as they go through their militant patrol, then there is ample time for musing. Mi tesoro de la sierra madre is sleeping snugly at my side. He is only naked and damp in the blanket I had the foresight to pack. I am rather glum though, for having swum the channel between Tom Sawyer Island and Fantasyland under the eye of Disney's futurizing moon, fleeing the insistent baying of increasingly proximate patrolhounds, not only my clothes but even my tobacco has become waterlogged, not to mention the forlorn wrinkles and curls on my padded leather pipe. The child, like a plush panda on his father's back, his arms resolutely round his father's waist, we bobbed like apples in the cold black waters of this festive themeworld. Now, thank God for it, five hours until dawn in Disney's kingdom, there's ample time for musing.

I remember that they used to call us café con leche. A brown person and his white querida strolling the barrio, or better yet, white astride his moto, fumando mota, white thighs and wacky white kneecaps flashing in the motorwake. Those were halcyon days: the miniskirt and unreconstructed integration. Los vatos were eyeing us with unconcealed envy. I was proud. "Orale, ése, ahí vienen, el café con leche. Hey man, I hear you're playing middle linebacker for State!"

The other morning I opened the post and saw Pancholín's scrawl on the verso of a Knott's Berry Farm postcard. I become tense when I get mail from my kid. I know it's going to basically govern my day. "Dear Daddy. I hope the cut on your cheek and the itsy-bitsy one on your nose is better now. I never see you much. The Creature Cantina you sent me se me rompió. I still love you but you're low on my loving list. First comes my mama, and then, Socorro, and then comes kitty-gato. Then comes YOU. Stephen comes to visit us a lot and stays over all nite. I love my mama all the way to the last number of counting. I love you too, but not as high. Pancholín."

That's what I get from beddy-bye, Kid Cappuccino, el mocha, the fruit of coffee with milk.

Well, that's it then, I thought, we're going to the beach. Only not there, because that muscle-bound oaf, Stephen, with his wriggling tattoo and his bionic pretensions probably lives with them both in a lean-to on muscle beach. I'll find someplace. I'm fed up with computing and permuting the parameters of bilingualism and wearied by the Feds with their ungracious timelines and audit trails. "You've never missed a deadline," my wife once said to me, "and it will kill you." Weird Hispanic Person. (Did you ever hear that joke: What's a Dry Martínez? A Mexican with a vasectomy!)

Actually it's not true at all. I've missed my share of deadlines. Lately, more than my share. I find the angst of impending loss flowering at the side of my self-correcting typewriter. I peer into the stereoscope for the hundredeth time and pass the experimental design:

PIE	PIE
DIME	DIME
COME	COME
HAY	HAY
ONCE	ONCE
SEA	SEA

One stimulus is going into the Hispanic eye, the other in the Anglo. The data base is moving under me like quicksand. This is something like mal de siècle. Frankly I don't know it it's mala fe, or merely mala leche.

I have a lab assistant who is very practical, and this is an invaluable asset. "Plain Jane," she calls herself, "the Carpenter's Dream Girl." I abhor this sort of gabacho masochism but in her somehow I tolerate it, and even empty my soul.

"Why don't you send for Mocha and have him down here

with you for a few days? Show him a good time, take him out to
search for fauna, maybe even go down to Disneyland?" She's
mixing coffee in a beaker. We do everything by sterotype in my
lab, you know, by the book. It helps me with my identity problem.
God knows, I'd wear a white lab coat if I could get away with it. Or
maybe one of those grand white chef's hats? But the students
would never stand for it. They'd laugh me out of Hilgard Hall. As
it is, the minute the temperature goes down a mite I put on my
three-piece corduroy suit with leather arm patches and light up
a briarwood, padded leather pipe.

I look at her with a sort of ironic leer, the kind that masks the
sort of hope you find in certain brown-skinned Catholics in Vegas,
who think that with the drunkenly solicited grace of God, they
can, in one definitive roll, come up with midnight at the Circus-
Circus. "How could I even consider taking a couple of days off
now? Aren't the Feds already muttering darkly about audit trails
and figuring maybe we jerked them off for a hundred grand in
computer upchuck?"

"Bah, come off it, Huitla. You're the senior Chicano in the
State system! With any luck at all the auditors'll find that un-
authorized trip to Tahoe and the University will have to bump
you up to dean."

I laughed. She's right about that. A little embarrassment
could be a great help at this point. I could leave behind the miasma
of unsynthesized detail and move into the upper reaches. The
deanship! A passport to the acme of thought.

"There you go then, schmendrik, it's settled."

"But wait. I can't take time off from my classes. You know
I never run out on my students. I'll have to wait 'til the trimester break."

"You don't teach on Friday, do you? Take a three-day blow.
Have you ever read that Hemingway tale? You could use a three-
day blow. Shit, I'll even fill in for your Friday afternoon tutorial.
You better decide quick before I change my mind."

Now we've come implacably to what is really the gist of the
matter. I look at her as if she were a creature demented. "What
are we talking about? You know I've already had him during this
trimester. That's the condition of the Consent Decree. I'm sur-
prised at you, Plain Jane, your own gabacho judge imposed that

condition. 'Look here, Huitla, once every trimester you get to have your son. That's plenty for your kind.' "

She chuckles. Pours milk into her coffee and eyes me like a shrewdy. "Well, maybe Linda will be cooperative. She just might look upon it differently this time. Circumstances do change, you know. Maybe she could use something of a healthy transition, seeing as how Stephen appears to have moved in."

Thanks, I needed that fact of life rubbed in my face. But I sure was pissed. "That California fruit fly, muscle bound maricón, hijo de la gran puta, mother-fucking no-good scum bag, hijo de un perro chirifusca. ¡Me cago en la leche que te han dado! ¡Me cago en tu estampa! ¡Me cago en el padre que te hizo! ¡Me cago en tu madre puta! ¡Me cago en tus muertos! ¡Me cago en la mar! ¡Me cago en la mierda! ¡Me cago en la porra! ¡Me cago en los cojones de Buda!" etc., etc.

Two weeks later I was at Linda's doorstep in Ventura. "Did you pack enough underwear for Kid Mocha this time? I don't want him to end up being a big chief gray pecker again!"

"Sure thing, perfesser. Can I get my A now?"

Pancholín bit my hand. "I'm no big chief gray pecker! That was for you, cukkamonga!"

"Ow, stop it. STOP IT! Look at my hand."

He swelled with glee. "Let me see it, Daddy. Are the teeth marks rising in your skin yet?"

"Look," said Linda. "I've got a couple of pieces of chicken in the refrigerator, some hardboiled eggs. I'll pack them up for you."

"No, don't bother."

"Why bother, right? They'd just compete with the junk food on the road."

"Sure. Taco Bell, Wendy's triples."

"Yeah. Burrito supremes. 'Hot and juicies.' "

"How come you're being so forthcoming?"

"I'm always forthcoming, Huitla. Too much so, that's how I get into trouble."

"I bet you could use these three days."

"I could use these three days."

"Is it that serious?"

"Not really."

"So it's that serious, huh? Mocha, go away. Play with your molded plastic toys. You heard me. Beat it! Scrambola!"

"Don't be a heavy, Huitla. Don't make me weary. It's as serious as it's ever going to be. It's not serious."

"How could you ever get mixed up with a tattooed beach bum like that?"

"You're really fucked up, you know that? He's only got one tattoo and it's on his arm. You make him sound like he came out of a Ray Bradbury story. Jesus Christ, why did I tell you about that tattoo? I suppose I get what I deserve."

"So when are you planning to get married?"

"I'm not thinking along those lines. But if *you* need a wedding ring I've got one you can have."

"Sure baby, thanks for the offer. Deep down you always thought I was basically your standard Hispanic troglodyte, didn't you, Linda? I mean, your typical A-frame Chicano structure, sure, with a veneer of Taco Bell and Lawn King dabbed on, an overlay, a glaze so to speak, a doctorate in scientific observation and measurement and the three-piece corduroy social life of the university, but down in the nitty-gritty, a romping pleistocene el macho."

"God save me from this. You promised, Huitla. You said you'd come up here and take Pancholín for a few days and give me a chance."

"Yes, I did. I'm sorry."

"We fell in love, we got married. And it was fine. But it didn't work out forever. There's no need to do this . . . this exercise in self-doubt and mortification. There was nothing . . . It was nothing that you point to on a good-bad scale. Just a lack of adjustment. A misfitting."

"Sure, like a tailor who messes up. You've told me a hundred times if you've told me once. A marriage that was a poorly tailored suit. Besides, who am I to complain of tattoos, didn't I use to drive you through the sal si puedes on my Harley Davidson?"

"That's right. Your skull and bones cycle."

"Sure, you remember that. Mostly I remember your knees, flashing white in the window panes of parked cars as we'd motor by. Jesus Christ, what woman wears a miniskirt on a motorcycle? ¡Y gringa! And los vatos, café con leche is what they called us. Hey man, here comes the strong coffee and his side of cream.

Remember how they'd make those barnyard kisses? I'd get pissed.
Ya estuvo, ¿no? Maricones de mierda. All fall down!"

"Huitla, come here. Sit down, I want you to know . . . and not
because this is so serious, because it isn't. It's just the first, you
know. And you need to adjust, and Pancholín too. But the odds
are one day there will be a serious one. I want you to know that
I loved you, and I still love you. It wasn't you or me either for
that matter. It wasn't culture or race or your personality. I love
you, but we couldn't . . . we couldn't live together forever after.
Life is just not like the fairytale. It was just a misfit. You've got to
believe that. It's really true."

"You mean, we were just too different?"

"Yes, too . . . like jigsaw pieces that don't really fit. They look
like they fit for a while. But then you go back to them and they
don't."

"Well, you're right there. Life ain't like no fairytale. That's for
sure. That's for fucking sure. What odds do you think Lloyd's of
London offers on mixed marriages?"

"Very low, I suppose. But that's got nothing to do with us.
That's not what did us in. Besides, we were only a partially mixed
marriage."

"Partially mixed! What in the hell are you talking about?"

"Well, we're both Catholic, aren't we?"

"Oh, sure, you in the Loew's Paramount in downtown St. Paul
converted into a cathedral with orchestra, loge and balcony seat-
ing, and me in an adobe chapel in the high sierra where you don't
bother to distinguish between the Christian godhead and the true
Quetzalcoatl! Tell me, you remember our trip to Turkey and
Greece? Do you agree that we conceived the kid in that Asian
watering hole somewhere on the road between Homer's Troy and
St. Peter's Ephesus, or do you still maintain that an accurate
backwards extrapolation of the days proves that conception was
while waiting for the damn plane to be ministered at the Roadway
Motor Hotel on 42nd Street almost under the gray West Side
Highway and the New York docks?"

"I see that's still bothering you."

"Yes, you might say it's paradigmatic."

"Well, have it your way, you can invent your little creation
myth if you like."

"No, seriously. I want to know your objective thinking on this matter."

"You know what I think. I'm sorry it disappoints you, but I was counting. That was my count. You should understand that. You're a researcher."

"Oh sure, a count is a count. How come when I count I go back to the ottoman in Balikesir?"

"That's because you don't make the full count. You refuse to add in the days that I was actually late."

"How do you know you were late in bearing? Couldn't it be my way, that we conceived two weeks later?"

"That's romantic Huitla, and mythical, but it's just not true. I was late. He was holding on for dear life. Inside me."

"Well, you're right there. Life is no fairytale. That's for sure, for fucking sure. You're always right, Linda. A total misfit. A marriage like a poorly tailored suit. Except for el mocha, let's call it a wash."

Finally, we are on the open road, shuttling down Highway 1. Coming up is Las Tunas beach. I know this area well. I used to own a bike.

Pancholín is playing tensely with his fingers. "Is there really an Order of the Golden Carp, or are you just making it up like the rest of your stories?"

"I never make up stories."

"Oh yeah? What about your dumb dromedary?"

"My dromedary is real."

"Then how come I can never see it?"

"You've seen him in a zoo. Also a Bactrian. But you haven't seen *my* dromedary because you don't believe in my beautiful dromedary and you only abuse him. You can only see him if you believe in him."

"That's what you always say. I bet your dromedary is not so beautiful. I bet he's ugly. I bet he's got poop on his bottom."

"No wonder you can't see him."

"I want to see him. Bring him here. I'll give him a punch right in the hump."

"No way!"

"I do believe in him! Hey, dromedary, listen! I believe in you . . . I believe in YOUUUUUU . . ."

"He doesn't believe you."

"That's what you always say. You don't have any dromedary. And there's no dromedary that spies on me at school and tells you what I do. You've got a dromedary, all right. It's in your head. That's all that it is. A dromedary in your head, but it's not real. And that goes for your golden carp too, and all your other cukka-monga made-up stuff."

"My dromedary told me you were playing in front of the school with Rick the other day and you lost your shoe in a pile of leaves and you had to go around without a shoe like a barefoot contessa until the assistant principal took you out at lunch period to find it."

"How did you know that?"

"My dromedary told me."

"Where was he?"

"Looking at you and Rick from behind the jungle gym."

"I bet Mommy told you."

"No, she didn't."

"Yes she did."

"No, she didn't!"

"Yes she did! She told you and not any silly dromedary what if it's real only lives in a zoo."

"Does your mommy know what you and Rick were playing in those leaves?"

"No."

"Well, I do."

"What?"

"Star Wars."

"How'd you know that?"

"Not only Star Wars. You were playing that you were in the garbage compactor."

"Who told you that?"

"My dromedary. He was a witness."

Pancholín became quiet. He pondered the facts. "I bet you just figured it out cause you're smart. You're a pretty smart daddy but you've got dromedaries in your head."

"You don't believe me?"

"I only believe in dromedaries when I see them."

"Then you can't see my dromedary. Because you've got to believe in him first. Then you can see him."

"Stop teasing me. Mommy says you're always teasing me!"

"She said that? Look, I'll tell you what I'm going to do. I'll let my dromedary drive the car. I'll take my hands off the wheel and he'll drive."

"You mean he's here now? Where is he?"

"In my lap."

"I can't see him." Pancholín carefully probed the space above my lap with his hand. "I don't feel a thing."

"Naturally. How are you going to feel an invisible creature? He's an ethereal dromedary."

"What's he doing?"

"He's getting ready to drive the car. He smells of desert spices, of myrrh and frankincense. He's just got back from the Sheeba shuttle. Okay, drom. Do your thing!" I took my hands off the wheel.

"Look, Dad, the car's moving!"

The car went straight for a while, then it began to veer off the road. I took back the wheel.

"Boy, some dromedary. Your camel drives just like a drunken dromedary."

"I think he did okay."

"You would. You're always sticking up for him. How come you always stick up for him?"

"I think he did pretty good for an animal with hooves. You should be grateful that you've got fingers and thumbs to grab. How would you like to drive a car with hooves?"

"Hmph! Why don't you stop here so we can go out on the beach?"

"You want to go for a swim?"

"No, I want to have a wrestle right on the sand."

"You think you're pretty tough, don't you."

"No, but I can sure beat you up."

"Oh yeah, tough guy?"

"That's for sure!"

"Only because you pull hair. That's no fair. No pulling hair. Then we'll see."

"What about you, cheater-chiter? You're always giving me lamb leg. That's no fair either."

"All right then. Maybe we'd better not wrestle. Your mommy's right. I tease you too much."

"Aw, c'mon Daddy, please. Please? I wanna wrestle."

We drove some more. You could see the beach and the gray waves curling like tongues from time to time off the road's enticing angles.

"Okay, punk," Pancholín said, "you've asked for no hair pulling, you got it!"

Immediately I veered off the road and down a sider. We parked tilting crazily against a sand dune.

"Oh boy! A wrestle!"

"Wait a second!"

"What?"

"I forgot something. Let's see your fingernails."

He hid his hands behind his back.

"No inspection, no wrestle."

We sat glowering at each other for a while. Finally, he showed them.

"Jesus Christ! They're worse than Dracula's!"

"I swear I won't gouge. I swear it on dromedary poop!"

"No way! Either I cut your nails or no wrestle. Do you know what my students said to me last time I came into class with my face all scratched up by your claws? They accused me of wrestling with a coed!"

"You can't cut them. You cut them too close. You stink! You make me bleed! I want my mommy to cut them!" He was teary, working himself up into a froth.

"Then forget it, punk. I knew you'd chicken out somehow."

On that note he gave in and presented his claws for trimming. I took the clipper from the glove compartment and worked as quickly and carefully as possible. He winced with every clip although it surely didn't hurt. When it was over he inspected each finger solicitously for blood or for tender pinkness.

"C'mon, Oedipus, time for the beach. Last one there is a squishy tamale. You gonna put on a bathing suit or you want me to throw you in the water with all your clothes on?"

"Don't call me any names, you little son of a bitch. I'll rip the hair out of your head."

The Wrestle is a formal ritual. It contains elaborate rules of redress. There is ample provision for the conjuring up of allies such as bumble horrors and Spider Man, Darth Vader, or in the father's case, the Cisco Kid. There is also occasion to act out

favored roles, to bring into service such useful adjuncts as force
fields, laser rays, karate chops, or when on a beach, fistfuls of
plentiful sand. The overall composition generally follows the
sonata form. There is, for example, the initial exposition of the
characters of father and son, replete with situation-specific braggadocio and a variety of feints, dodges, ruses and ploys, and even an
occasional scuffle. The development stage is often signaled by
ritualized contrapuntal verbal abuse whereby the antagonists are
serially baited and goaded with a variety of epithets derogatory
of wrestling valor such as Chicken Chartreuse, Chicken Chow
Mein, punky Cukkamonga, el moco verde, el grande de pavo,
esquinkel (*vid.* esquintle, Nahuatl), kid moco, el creepo, nothing
but a pigeon, *et alia.* At this point physical contact begins to in-
crease in intensity and range and becomes characterized by a
variety of holds, locks, grips and pins, together with rabbit punch-
es, bites, kicks, tumbles, karate chops, hair-pulling, gouging,
scratching, and pinching. Soon, immersed in this embattled frenzy,
one is wont to seek the succor of allies with supernatural or
mythical powers. Or better yet, to become one of these transcen-
dent beings oneself. "Ha, ha! And now punk, Dr. Precision is
going to get you with his horse needle!" With respect to deep
narrative structure, The Wrestle often takes its cue from the
earlier lore of Westerns. The father is conscious of this, the son is
unaware; yet they play it out orthodoxly, even as the surface
language reflects the faddish advances of the space age. The good
guy (white hat, never a Meskin, except maybe for the Cisco Kid)
is beaten up mercilessly while at the same time tormented like
Christ on his Calvary (harking back to an even earlier lore), until the inciting moment. This pivotal point in The Wrestle is repre-
sented by an outrage above and beyond all previous outrages
incorporated into the ritual. Thus the crucial element of the outrage gives to The Wrestle a certain open-endedness, a sense of
heretofore unexamined peril, a quality of advancement or additiv-
ity, in what otherwise might be considered a closed and self-con-
tained system. On the occasion in question, the outrage is exempli-
fied by the father (the bad guy) holding the son (the good guy)
upside down over the surf, and threatening to throw him in fully
clad, moreover actualizing the threat by occasionally dunking the
good guy's head into three inches of surf while firmly holding him
like a seven-year-old Ulysses, by the heels.

Once having somehow "miraculously" broken the outrage, the good guy, swollen with righteous indignation, a moral imperative highlighted in vehemence by the intensity of the very travesty of the outrage itself, takes heavily to task the bad guy, who is thrown from bound to bound and torn limb from limb. Hence we proceed to recapitulation; it is the child overcoming his daddy, all the time assuring him he's nothing more than the Chicken Chartreuse, el punko green snot, grande pavo esquinkel, double deer-crossing with three-in-one oil, high rating on the turkometer, that he has claimed for the daddy all along. Closure is achieved swiftly enough, about four or five times after the daddy issues the incantation, "I give up!" and often with a culminating fistful of pulled hair and a boot in the ass.

We didn't get in until late that night what with The Wrestle, and after that a swim and some chow at a roadside dump called the Doggy Diner. Even Pancholín, who isn't particularly fond of the sedentary life, wanted to rest and muse and ponder. He took off his socks and inspected his toes with a sort of inquisitiveness that reminded me of the days when he was just a baby and first discovered them. "Think there was any golden carp in that ocean we were swimming in?"

"Naw. Carp is a freshwater fish."

"Well, maybe there was some silver carp in there. What about silver carp, are they freshwater or salt?"

"Silver carp? There aren't any silver carp. Just gold. The golden carp is a fish that once was a god. The other gods were sick to death of the sinning of their people and they turned them into carp to live forever in the river, but there was one kind god, who was so saddened by this, and so afraid for his people, that he asked that he too be turned into a carp to be near them and look over them. This is the golden carp."

"And who were the people, Daddy?"

"The people, Pancholín? They would be . . . the Chicano people."

Pancholín smiled broadly. "Like me, right Daddy? I'm a Chicano person."

"Right, like you."

"Only I'm not only a Chicano. I'm a gabacho too."

"Yes, only that's not such a pretty word. You don't have to use that word."

"Well, Chicano isn't such a pretty word either. Some kid up at school called me a lousy Chicano half-breed so I had to beat his ass. Only he was a pretty tough turkey. He was a grade higher."

"Chicano is a nice word for Chicanos. And that's what counts."

"And gabacho is a nice word for gabachos, and that's what counts."

"Only it doesn't work like that. Chicanos call Chicanos, Chicano. But gabachos don't call each other that. Gabacho is a word that Chicanos use for gabachos."

"Don't Chicanos like gabachos?"

"Sometimes they do and sometimes they don't."

"But they don't always like them?"

"Naw, not always. Hell, Chicanos don't always like Chicanos."

"But you're Chicano, right Daddy? And Mommy is gabacha, right?"

"Sort of. I don't like the word you're using."

"Never mind that. You used to like each other a lot. Now, you don't like each other that much."

"But it's got nothing to do with what kind of people we are. We just didn't fit well together."

"But how come Stephen stays over all the time? Stephen's a gabacho, right? Why doesn't Mommy love another Chicano, like you?"

"Would that make it any easier? Your mommy says she still loves me. She just doesn't want to live with me anymore. We still love each other. Besides, she's not in love with Stephen. She told me so this morning. She told me it's nothing serious. Besides, there's not so many Chicanos in this world. We're few and far between. Besides, she loves you, doesn't she? And you're Chicano, right? Besides, I don't like that word, gabacho."

"Okay, then, big shot professor. What word should I use?"

"Use a word that they use for themselves, not one that we use for them."

"Well, like what?"

"I don't know, there's plenty of them. Like white."

"White? You mean the color white?"

"Sure, your mother is white, isn't she?"

"Yeah, she's not only white. She's pure white like a glass of milk."

"And I'm more like coffee-colored, right?"

"Yeah."

"And you, you're a color that's like when you mix coffee and milk, right?"

"Yeah."

"Well, there you go. You're all set."

He thought for a while. "The guy in school, you know, the one who gave me a popeye? He was black."

"Hmmm. Well, he's got his own problems. I can see why he might not like Chicanos. He's a special case."

"Yeah, maybe." Pancholín thought about it some more. "Isn't there another word for gabacho, instead of white? I don't think that word works so good. Only with Mommy because she's really white, the whitest thing that ever lived. Nobody else I know is white. There's plenty of gabachos around who are red looking with red noses or yellow looking, kind of brown, and black and chocolate."

". . . and green and purple too, right kid? Okay, here goes another one for you. Gabachos like to think of themselves as American."

"American? But you're American, aren't you? And you're not gabacho."

"Yes, but I'm Mexican-American, see the difference?"

"Then what am I?"

"Well, you would be Mexican-American; American-American. See what I mean?"

"I'm not too sure. Is there another word?"

"How about Anglo? There's another one for you."

"Anglo? Nah. That's not right. That's when two lines come together. They make an Anglo."

"No, you mean angle. I mean Anglo."

"Are you sure?"

"Well, maybe when I grow older I'll use Anglo. But you know what I think I want to do now?"

"No, what?"

"I want to use gabacho. But I want everybody to know I don't mean it nasty. I even use it for myself."

"Okay, then. It's settled, at least for now. It sounds like your daddy when he was young. He used Mexican, but he wanted everybody to know he was the faithful Mexican, the one that saved the sheeprancher's daughter, and not the perfidious one that . . . uh, did her wrongful harm."

"I'm sleepy, Daddy. Can I sleep here on the couch?"

"I'll carry you. I've got your bed all made."

I put him in the bed. He stretched out his hands and I bent down and kissed him.

"I love you, Daddy. A lot-lot."

"I love you too, pumpkin, all the way to the last number of counting."

"When I grow up I'm going to college and become a professor and learn all about words."

"You know what?" I said to him. "I think you've just made my day." Only I wasn't sure if he heard me because Pancholín falls asleep so fast.

About 7:00 a.m. Pancholín was in my room, making weird noises. He wouldn't wake you up exactly, he knew he wasn't supposed to disturb his daddy. But he'd play in the room. First, he'd start with a whisper. He'd re-create intergalactic battles and summon the Incredible Hulk and Wonder Woman to his side. By 7:30 the whispers had given way to loud zaps and rata-tat-tats as ray guns and stun pistols reverberated from the legions of molded plastic figurines that were propped strategically around the bedroom.

"You want breakfast?"

"What you got?"

"I've got Rice Krispies. I've got Cheerios. Take your pick."

"You mean you don't have Count Chocula?"

"You know I don't keep that sugary garbage around. Your mother lets you eat that stuff?"

"No."

"Well, then?"

"I was just asking."

"Boy, when I was your age all I got was a cup of black coffee and a stale bolillo. Then I had to work all day hunting for tin cans and scrap metal."

"That must have been funnnnnnnnnn. You know what? I want both. Rice Krispies and Cheerios all mixed up. Say, Daddy, do you think we could send away for this magic ring? Only two box tops and twenty-five cents."

"I've got something better than that for you." I opened the top drawer of the chest and took out my Phi Beta Kappa key. "See this!"

"Wow! It's gold, isn't it?"

"Sure!"

"Is it pure gold? Or is it just gold on top like what rubs off?"

"Pure gold!"

"Wow! What is it?"

"It's the sacred key to the Order of the Golden Carp."

"Is that what I get if I make Carp First Class?"

"None other."

"And what am I now? A tadpole, right?"

"Right. But if things go well, by tomorrow you'll be a Carp First Class."

"What are you, Daddy? What class carp are you? Second? Third? Ninth?"

"No, you're going the wrong direction. First is the highest of the classes. Me, I'm a . . . a Goldfish Supreme."

"Is that the highest?"

"Oh, that's definitely the highest. As a matter of fact, I'm one of the senior carps in the system."

"Oh boy, the highest number of counting of carps. What comes after Carp First Class?"

"Well, uh, there's Star, and then, Life, and then, Goldfish Supreme."

"But why a goldfish? I thought you was a carp!"

"Yeah, well, I am. Goldfish is another word for carp. Only it's the secret word. You're not gonna tell anybody, are you?"

"Naw. I won't tell anybody, except for other carps. Who else is a carp, Daddy?"

"Who else? Well . . . uh . . . all the Chicanos. All the Chicanos who make the grade that is. If you ask one and he doesn't know what you're talking about then you can be sure they've passed him by and he's nothing more than a Chicken Chartreuse es-quinkel."

Pancholín fell down laughing. "Right! Right!" Then he turned serious. "What about Mommy? Is she one?"

"Well, not exactly. She approves of them though. She's a corresponding member of the academy."

"Why don't we start up a Silver Carps? For mommies and girls."

"Not a bad idea. Maybe we should bring it up in August. You know, on the convention floor."

"Tell me again, Daddy. What do I have to do to be a Carp First Class?"

"Well, lots of things."

"Like what?"

"Lots of things. You'll find out as we do them. But every First Class Carp has got to do these two things. One, he's got to find a treasure. And two, he's got to spend the night out-of-doors, in a scary place."

"Yikes! And we're gonna spend it on Tom Sawyer Island, in the old cave!"

"Right you are, none other."

"Yikes!"

"You're not scared, are you?"

"Naw. You'll be there, right?"

"Definitely."

"Think there's any bats in that cave?"

"I'll have the dromedary scare them away."

Pancholín looked at me dubiously.

"Think there are any snakes in that cave?"

"Naw. Snakes like to snuggle into little holes and crevices, kind of like kitty-gato does. Caves are more for big game like wolves and bears."

"Yikes! Maybe the six wolves all live in the cave."

"What six wolves?"

"You know. The wherewolf, the whatwolf, the which, the when, the why, and the whowolf."

"Oh, those guys. Those are just made-up wolves. Those are wh-wolves. They wouldn't be in Tom Sawyer's Cave."

"I thought they were real wolves! You see, you make up everything! I know the wherewolf is real. I've seen him on T.V."

"So it's real if you've seen it on T.V.? Never mind that anyway. We've got to get ready." I brought the gear that I'd stowed away for the outing. "Think we've got everything?"

"Oh boy! A flashlight! Can we make animals with our fingers against the wall of the cave?"

"Hey, that's a great idea! We'll do all kinds of fun things."

"Wanna see my rabbit? I make a beautiful rabbit. ¡Mira qué precioso!"

"Not now. In the cave."

"You know what? You're missing one thing."

"What would that be?"

"A weapon."

"Nah, we don't need a weapon. We'll vanquish any enemies we may encounter with our bare hands."

"Suppose they've got dogs?"

"Dogs at Disneyland? Nah, they wouldn't do that."

"Why don't you pack some hamburger with sleeping drugs in it? If some dogs come around we'll give them a little snooze." Pancholín chortled.

"Pretty good idea. Only I don't have any sleeping drugs and who wants to carry around some smelly old raw meat in a knapsack all day?"

By 8:00 p.m. we were on our last legs. We had done it all, especially anything that whirred, whipped, whirled, whined, whistled or whizzed (six wh-'s over Disney) including the Jungle Cruise, Star Jets, Grand Prix Raceway, 20,000 Leagues Under the Sea, Snow White's Scary Adventures, Dumbo the Flying Elephant, The Mad Tea Party and Mr. Toad's Wild Ride.

As darkness came upon us Pancholín grew more and more apprehensive. It was a typical syndrome of his so I didn't pay it that much mind. We went back to the locker where we stowed away the knapsack and we got it out.

"Daddy, you remember those hippos and alligators on the Jungle Cruise? That's not the water around our island, is it?"

"Not at all. They keep those big lugs out of the way of the paddlewheeler. Besides, you're not scared of those silly guys? They're no more real than your Creature Cantina or Luke Skywalker. Giant hunks of molded plastic, that's what they are."

Pancholín was dubious, very dubious.

"Well my man, the last vessel moves out in five minutes. Which will it be, Tom Sawyer's Rafts or Captain Fink's Keel Boats?"

Pancholín sighed. "We might as well take the Keel Boats. They look safer."

On the boat he began whimpering and rubbing his eyes, all the while making a herculean effort to hold in the tears. "Do we have to spend the whole night on this silly island? I'm cold!"

"Pancho! Be quiet! You want everybody to know our business? My God, it's the hottest night in the valley. Besides, I packed a blanket."

"Are you sure there's no bats in that cave? Maybe dogs go in there and pee on the floor."

"They don't let dogs in Disney's land. No way."

"Well, we're not supposed to stay in here after dark. What'll they do with us if they catch us?"

"Maybe they'll throw us in that pirate's dungeon over in Adventureland."

He started whimpering some more. "You're always teasing me. Why don't you stop teasing me?"

"I'm sorry. I tell you what. We'll go to the island and visit Fort Mark Twain and fire the rifles and explore the caves for bats. If you want to stay, fine, and if you don't, pues, ¡qué carajo! ¡Fuímonos!"

"And if we go, do I still get to have the Order of the Golden Carp?"

"You know I can't do that. But you can always try again next year when you're a bigger boy."

Pancholín sighed again like the weight of the world and his culture was on him, but by the time we had explored each and every path on the island, each crevice and cave or mine shaft, each sharpshooter's niche and the secret tunnel out of the fort, he was singing a different tune, like I figured he would.

"This place is neat! Can we sneak up to the lookout after everybody leaves?"

"Maybe, if it seems safe."

Soon enough the bell came for the last raft to leave the island. We slipped away and hid way in the bowels of Old Jim's Cave, "quiet like mouses."

"Ya se van, ¿verdad?"

"Pues sí, gringos mensos. ¡Que aquí hay dos chicanitos escondidos de deveras!"

"Papi, ¿ya nos podemos salir?"

"Todavía no. Mira, aquí voy a tender la manta. Acuéstate un ratito. Vamos a hacer animalitos con la luz del flashlight. Ya te diré cuando podemos salir a regir la islita."

"Yo quiero ser el rey. No, mejor el principe. Que tú seas el rey."

"¡Andale pues! Pero por ahora quietito como si fueras la momia de la cueva de Drácula."

We must have been playing in the cave for at least an hour or two. It was so quiet and peaceful. We had ventured out and filled up two pillow cases I had packed with leaves and grass. We were all set. I even considered making a fire, but then thought twice about it.

"Do you want to know why I tease you a little?"

"Yeah. Why?"

"Because sometimes we play in a way that we're like brothers. You know, I had lots of brothers. And we teased each other a lot. I teased them and they teased me. There was Pancracio and Curro and Tecolote and Joselito-Joey and . . ."

"How come you don't still tease your brothers?"

"Never see them anymore. Curro's been dead 15 years now. Tecolote's designing hydraulic screws for the space project, Pancracio and Joselito still hauling scrap metal . . ."

"How come I don't have any brothers?"

"You were going to have some. Your mommy and I were planning to, but we didn't get the time."

"Why would you tease your brothers?"

"Because they teased me."

"Well, I don't tease you, but you still tease me."

"I guess so. The trouble is, once you're a teaser then you're always stuck a teaser. Es un vicio como cualquier otro. I'll try not to tease you so much."

"You'd better. Cause if not maybe I'll pull some more hair out of your head. Why'd the cops shoot your brother?"

"¡Qué sé yo! I wish I knew. Some cops don't like people who look too dark. When you're an older boy we'll have to talk about that more. Ley fuga. Or maybe cause they figured they couldn't pin a rap on him in court."

"What's a rap?"

"When they say you've done something wrong."

Then we heard a sound from outside. We heard it again, a dog barking, a little closer.

"What are we going to do?" Pancholín asked.

"Jesus, I wish I had that poison meat." I packed up our gear. "We've got to make tracks."

"Daddy! Let's go to the Tree House. We'll be way up in the tree. Nobody'll get us there."

"That's a damn good idea. Only one problem, we've got to get across this channel. Look, you wait here! I'm going to swim across and untie the raft and bring it back here."

"No way! If you're swimming out of here, I'm swimming with you."

I could see he was determined. "Look, I'll just be back in a minute. You don't want to get soaked. I'll be right back with the nice dry raft."

"No way!"

"You're going to come with me in the water?"

"Uh huh!"

"You swear to God you'll never tell Mommy!"

"I swear. I swear to God and hope to die."

The dog barked. It was too close for comfort.

"Yikes! We've got to get out of here. You grab my waist real tight. We're going to walk in the water. No heroic stuff now. Nice and easy, walking in the water. That's right, nice and easy."

Halfway across the channel, I asked him, "Feel any fish nibbling at your leg?"

"No. Do you?"

"No, but if you do, don't worry. They're friendly carp."

"Okay."

We were on the other side in a jiffy. We hid in the wooden boathouse where the customers queue up for the rafts. We peered over the rim. Two patrolmen were coming, one from each direction. We ducked down into the shadows of the hut.

"Hey, Bud," one said to the other, "you on again tonight?"

"Yeah, third night in a row Disney sticks me with the graveyard shift. See anything exciting?"

"What's to see? Minnie Mouse's underpants? Say, Bud. What's the matter, somebody over in the central office don't like you?"

"I don't know. Maybe so."

"You better watch over your old lady, Bud. Somebody in central's got you on graveyard duty." The guard walked away, chortling all the while.

Bud stopped and lit a cigarette. He flicked the match our way and cursed Donald Duck's mother. Then he moved on.

Once they were gone we could hardly suppress our mirth, even soaked as we were.

"Can you believe that? Can you believe it!"

"What a guard, Papi! ¡Qué loco! He looks up Minnie Mouse's dress! ¡Es el más grande de todos los guajolotes!"

While Pancholín wasn't looking I planted on the ground a silver five-peso piece, un Hidalgo that I had gotten as a present when I was a kid and which had been rattling around the bottom drawer for three decades. "You know what? I think you must be the bravest kid in the valley. I've got a mind to buck you straight up to Star."

"Star! Wow! But I haven't even found a treasure."

"Gee, that's right. That's too bad. Say, what's that silvery flashing thing?"

"Look, Daddy. It's a silver coin." Pancholín grabbed for it. "It's the biggest silver coin in the world!"

"It sure looks like it. What does it say?"

"It says cinco pesos."

"Do you know what that means?"

"Yeah, five bucks."

"Yeah, but it means it's Chicano money. It's a Chicano treasure!"

"How did it get here?"

"Maybe somebody originally buried it here for good luck. Or maybe . . ." I look over to the water.

"The carp, right Daddy?"

"I don't know."

"Maybe it's the carp that shot it up here out of the water."

"I don't know. Let's go look."

We looked into the water, long and hard. There was nothing. We looked and looked. Then there was a ripple out in the channel.

"He's out there all right," Pancholín said. "The carp that looks out for Chicanos." We both shivered with that incisive sense of revelation that only young children can experience.

"Okay," I said. "We're moving out to the Swiss Family Tree House."

We crossed the lighted walkway into the unlit bosom of shrubbery, first one, then the other, like guerrillas on assignment. Carefully we made the journey to Adventureland. Then over the puny fence and up the staircased Swiss Family Tree, platform by platform and tree-room by tree-room to the topmost platform. We took off our clothes and hung them to dry. Pancholín wrapped himself in the blanket. We looked down from the treecrown on the Magic Kingdom. Main Street was all lit up and so was Cinderella's Castle. Above, starry heavens capped the sultry night and in the channel prescient carp bided the golden dawn. All was well in the valley.

"Ready to sleep?"

"Yes. I love you Daddy, all the way to the last number of counting."

We hugged and kissed and Pancho went to sleep and I sat up looking out from the tree, thinking warm thoughts about the great chain of being, especially of my father who during one period of his life raised geese to be industrial watchdogs and the way he carried on the day I got that fellowship, my mother in the background, biting her fingers, scared to death and with reason, because I'd be breaking the cycle of tirilones, pachucos and pochos, with their papiamento of street caliche and devious calques, and emerging into the alienating, mainstream Other. God knows, even she had no inkling then I would fall in love with and marry una del otro estirpe. And the walks we took in the barrio past the chicharronería ("sin pelos, ¿eh?"), past the molino de nixtamal, past El Mandamás del Barrio, a beer for my father and a nieve to sweeten my mouth. My father with his moral paradigms, the Chicano Aesop discussing the virtue of geese. "Never take for granted other persons or animals, you must always work toward them, make great effort, is like fine art, a ritual of love." He rolled up his sleeve. "You see this scar on my arm? You see that, the patrón made me go and get it stitched today because it didn't want to heal. You know Doña Jacinta, the big she-goose? She's the one I trained first, she's been with me as a watchdog now for over four years. And what a fine guardian she is. She will hiss like a siren and peck out the eyes of any stranger unless she's well leashed.

But last week I got careless. Who knows what I did, walked in this manner instead of that, failed to greet her in my usual soothing way, had on a funny hat, most of all I forgot that she had just hatched goslings who were under the wooden stairs. Before I know it, peck, peck and my arm was damn near sliced off before she recovered form and hid herself in shame. But it's my fault, I say. I tell the patrón I well deserved this moral lesson, because love is not a cheap commodity. It must be won time and over again."

As often occurs with me, moral quandries rise up from their repressed bottleneck and beset me just as I fall asleep. I remember thinking that on the one hand it was deceitful to have fixed a false mythos on Pancholín with a silver Hidalgo, on the other the fix or rather feelings were real, and as Thomas Merton had once said (I paraphrase), mysticism was nothing more than the concerted return to the childhood condition of feckless faith. Ultimately it was good, I thought or dreamt, to care or feel deeply.

"Hey, motherfucker! What do you think you are? Some kind of tree house owl?"

I woke up groggy. The sun was just over the barranca and in my eyes.

"Say, these brown boys are in their birthday suits."

"Look, gentlemen, we got lost in the cave over on the island. We heard some dog barking and we swam over here."

"Yeah, I bet. Just who the hell are you? The Frito Bandito? And while you're answering, stick out your hands for these cuffs."

"I won't do that."

"What do you mean, Pancho? You won't do WHAT?"

"Take it easy, fella. I'm going to put on my clothes now, nice and easy. Then I'm gonna go with you just where you say. Don't get my son riled up."

"¡No te dejes, papi! ¡No te dejes!"

"You're gonna do what I tell you, boy, and that means these sturdy cuffs!" The guard raised his stick menacingly.

"¡No te dejes, papi! ¡No te dejes!"

The other guard looked through my pants and my watery wallet. "Say, Bubba, take it easy on this sumbitch. He's some kind of perfesser. We'd better get the P.R. man."

"¡No te dejes, papi! ¡No te dejes! ¡No te dejes! ¡No te dejes! ¡No te dejes! ¡No te dejes!"

"That was some fool thing to do!"

"Oh yes, I'll grant you that. But it did have its culminating moments."

"I bet, Mr. Macho. I know, you used to own a bike. What's the matter with you, anyway? You going through a premature climacteric? You getting hot flashes?"

"Maybe so. I'm quijotesque. You're never going to believe this, but it was my hispano way of expressing my great love for you and our son."

"How flattering. Getting booked for trespassing and indecent exposure just for us. Next time spare us the flaco favor."

"Kid Mocha, he was magnificent, you know that? I'm thinking of bucking him straight up to Star in the Grand Order of the Golden Carps."

"Swell! That's great. On his police record let it read that he proceeded straight to Star in the Golden Carps!"

"You're not going to believe this, but you know what started it? His toy, se le rompió. Gabo's deluxe, all Star Wars shiny with fourteen blinking lights and seven discrete functions. And a grand total of six D-size alkaline power cells just to run. What to do? What to do?"

"What in God's creation are you talking about?"

"I'm talking about the unconditionally secure toy." (The ultimate toy, with a self-replenishing warranty. Poor shook up child, all your toys seem to give prematurely.) "Stuck with a bad daddy, and not enough of him at that. Reminds me of Woody's old joke about how bad the food is and besides there's not enough of it. Linda, please don't go to the judge."

"I won't do that. I won't go to the judge."

"Bless you. I'll be good from now on. So help me God, I'll be good."

"Yeah, I bet you will."

"I will, I will! Swear to God and hope to die. From now on I'm the faithful Mexican. Wait and see. Is it serious?"

"What?"

"You and the tattooed man."

"About the same."

"With you everything is always, about the same."

"That's right. I haven't gotten to your point of hot flashes yet. What is Disney going to do?"

"Disney's not half bad. Anybody who could do a Bambi can't be all that bad."

"Are they going to prosecute you?"

"I don't think so. I think we'll sit down together and sign some sort of Consent Decree. Otherwise it would be poor press to go after me, don't you think? 'Weirdo professor and son booked for spending night in Disney Tree House?' I don't think they would want that kind of attention. God knows, on that basis tomorrow night they could have a hundred stowaways. There'd be people sneaking down the plastic hippo's mouth."

"I hope you're right. Supposing they do prosecute? What'll the University do to you?"

"To me? They'd probably make me a Dean. It would be an affirmative action. The University's so dizzy, who could tell? A Disneyland of the mind, to paraphrase a poem I know. Who could tell, with a little student rallying I could end up . . . God knows, look what happened to Hayakawa."

"Yeah, I've heard it. You used to own a bike, and now you're the senior carp in the river. Some success story. Somehow your circumstances and Hayakawa's don't seem quite comparable to me. Non Sequitor, Huitlacoche."

"Well, then, what about tenure? I've got tenure."

"Does it cover moral turpitude?"

"A little flashing in a tree house? There's a moral here for sure, but it ain't turpitude. Look, I'm trying to figure out what I did and why I did it. Get a researcher's handle on it, if you know what I mean. I had fallen low on the loving list. Low on the ratings. This is California. Everyone's for a guy on the comeback trail. All I wanted to do was place a little higher. To rise a bit in esteem. Perhaps to be loved all the way to the last number of counting. That's all it was. It was an affirmative action."

we, the cultural workers of
MAIZE
are appreciative of the generous support of the National Endowment
for the Arts and for the in-kind services that the Centro Cultural de la
Raza in San Diego, California, and The Colorado College in Colorado
Springs have provided for these publications. The contents of our publications are the sole responsibility of the authors and editors and in no
way reflect the particular policies and opinions of the sponsors.